THANKS YO[U] HELPING TO MAKE THIS A REALITY

[signature]

1/9/13

THANKS FOR
HELPING TO MAKE
THIS A BEAUTY

GG
1/9/15

HUMANITY GONE

BOOK I

AFTER THE PLAGUE

BY

DEREK DEREMER

WITH DEAN CULVER

This is a work of fiction. Any resemblance to actual events, locales, organizations, or persons, living or dead, is entirely coincidental.

© 2012 by Derek Deremer

Editing by Sandra Finley

Prologue

So this is what the world has become.

Bullets continue to tear through the other side of the car. The small explosions and ricochets cement my feet tighter to the asphalt and I press as close as I can to the outside of the driver's side door. Every muscle in my body aches, but I know that I cannot give up here. She needs me. More than that, I promised my dad I would keep her safe. But most of all, I swore to myself that I would never let anything happen to her, no matter what it took. It was an odd promise for a seventeen year old to make at the time. A bullet shatters through the window above me and showers me with glass. I reach to my neck and swipe the shards away, cutting both my neck and hand in the process.

Warm blood runs down my spine and I see a puncture on my left hand. Red droplets fall to the street.

If I don't move now, they are going to kill me.

I glance behind me to where the twins are hiding over the hill. I imagine they are still as I left them, huddled together with tears in their eyes. When I had first charged into the fray, they screamed at me to stop, and their screams continued for a while, but were barely audible when I went over the hill. Any noises from them would be completely gone amidst the chaos.

Could they have been found already? Probably not. They are safe from these monsters' bullets on the other side of the hill. I am the one in danger. My sister is the one in danger.

Mustering up the courage, I quickly peer through the shattered glass toward the shooters. There are at least six boys in the house. Two hide behind a make-shift barricade of wood and brick on the front lawn and the others were peering out the house's already shattered windows. At least three of them have guns. I duck down just as another bullet embeds itself into the car's steel on the other side. They have me pinned down, and my only small hope is their need to reload. I use my bloodied hand to recheck the cylinder in my own gun. It only holds five shots, my only five shots, and it is not nearly enough. They have bigger guns. Most of all, I would be lucky enough to even hit the house with this thing.

I hate guns again...

A portion of the tire to my left is torn away by another flying bullet. What's left of the tire deflates and the car crashes down to the hubcap. I really hate guns.

The gunfire all of a sudden ceases. An eerie silence spreads over the lawn. My ears still ring from the noise of bullets, and the boys are shouting amongst themselves. I look up and notice all of the boys staring back at me. They have stopped firing, but my heart continues to the rhythm of the gunshots. What are they doing? Then I hear *his* voice. His rusty tone seems to echo off the asphalt street and stirs my insides. To think I trusted him.

"Is that really you ole' Johnny boy? Well if you want her this bad, I guess I could offer a trade."

Chapter 1: Jonathon

I turn up the volume on the television set. I had muted it as I finished my geometry work, but I took note of the banner across the bottom of the screen. I read it again and again. The information is nothing new, but I still find that my eyes fix themselves to the screen when they see the words:

...60 MILLION MORE DIE OF MYSTERIOUS ILLNESS...

Ever since last month, people have been mysteriously dying all over the country. It keeps getting worse, and people are getting more and more restless outside of our apartments. The news and the president keep reassuring everyone that it will be okay. And when I say president, I mean the new president. The first was one of the initial victims to the "mysterious illness." The vice president soon followed. I guess they had presidential succession for a reason.

It starts with a rash with blisters, and then evolves into a fever. Then the body burns up so badly that it shuts down. Scientists, they say, are trying, but no one can stop it. School was suspended indefinitely two weeks ago, but I find myself still doing math to ease my mind. When I am engulfed in a math problem, my mind temporarily stops worrying what will happen tomorrow, next week, next month. Or next year. If there will be a next year. Finishing my senior year looked bleak.

I move from the beige carpeting up into the comfort of the couch, bringing my work into my lap. My sister looks over from the dining room table. In front of her is a small cake she had prepared earlier that morning. Our dad loves the chocolate cake that my sister makes. She somehow added mint cookies to the recipe and it was to die for, but now it seems that someone is living for it. Our father woke up yesterday; a grotesque redness had emerged up from under his shirt and onto his neck. We had prayed that he wasn't going to get it. Today, he woke up with a 104 degree temperature. Now, he is resting in between vomiting episodes.

Tomorrow, he will be dead.

My sister found comfort in preparing the cake and possibly letting him enjoy it the best he could before he slipped away. I want, or rather we want, to do more, but we can't. The hospital is overwhelmed with patients and is no longer accepting anyone. Yesterday, I drove down and pleaded my case to the nurse at the front. After shoving through the sidewalks and pushing my way into the busy lobby, I made it to the hospital desk. She looked at me with sad eyes and just said, "Keep him comfortable." I hadn't been kidding myself; not even a single recorded patient had recovered. Every woman or man who took ill was dead within three days. Mysteriously however, no one under the age of nineteen has gotten sick. Not even a single child has fallen ill. My dad begged us to just drop him off at one of the Red Cross's "sick" tents that were up all over the city, but we refused. The tents were in pitiful condition and it was just somewhere else for him to die. We are going to stay a family as long as possible. It isn't going to be much longer anyway.

My sister, Jocelyn, sets down the icing and walks over behind me, placing her hands on the back of the couch. Jo, as dad and I call her, gazes at the television. The news has been trying to keep the country updated, but everyone is dying. On the screen, a newswoman looks back blankly at us. She seems to have more make-up than normal and beads of sweat roll down her face. Her teal blouse looks worn. She is dying too, but she works on. I imagine people like her are barely keeping the city together. Her words are labored as they escape her fatigued body:

"It has just entered the newsroom that another estimated sixty million deaths have been confirmed across the U.S. Some reports indicate this number is even higher. A rough poll seems to show that nine out of every ten adults is or has been infected and doctors believe all adults will succumb. Children have been shown resistant to the plague, even with direct exposure. Despite America still being in quarantine, foreign aid continues to pour in from Canada and the UK. However, they still aren't letting anyone leave the country and have set up military roadblocks along all major roadways. Unconfirmed reports have said that even patrols and fences have begun to appear at the border between these roads. Canada is not taking any chances on the disease spreading to its land. There are still no reported instances of the disease in any other country. Mexico, on the other hand, lacks the resources to prevent the mass immigration of children and unaffected adults into their country.

"If you or someone you love has become infected, the remaining doctors are encouraging you to stay at home. Hospitals are beginning to shut down across the nation as doctors and nurses are becoming scarce." The newscaster already seems tired from talking. She coughs. Her eyes turn from the camera to her left. She seems to be listening to someone. I share a glance with my sister before the newscaster returns her eyes to the screen. The newscaster's bloodshot eyes are now filled with tears.

"My manager has just informed me that this will be our last broadcast. Nearly all of us at the station, including myself, have begun to show symptoms. We have done our best to continue to keep you informed of the horrific events of this last month. We ask everyone to remain calm throughout the dark days ahead. To the young viewers, it will be okay. People are working around the clock to create a plan for you. Stay calm, and await help." She pauses momentarily, seemingly out of words. "May God be with all of you. Good-bye."

A tear flows down the side of her cheek as her composure finally gives in during her final words. She begins to cough. Then all of a sudden the television goes blank and an eerie pitch yells from the speakers. I fumble for the remote and turn it off. I feel Jocelyn's hand rest on the top of my head. Her fingers clench my hair tighter than she realizes. It hurts, but I don't say a word.

"What are we going to do?" she says. Her voice seems to be devoid of any emotion. I turn my head up and see her hazel green eyes between the bangs of red hair. Tear stains line her pale cheeks. These stains have not left since dad became sick. She keeps disappearing into her room and comes back with bloodshot eyes. She's a year younger than me, but she wants to look strong for me. I don't know how to answer her. I have been trying to figure out a plan ever since the news suggested yesterday that 99% of America's adults would be dead by the end of next week. No more cops, firefighters, doctors, or utility workers. I know that we need a plan.

The city is going to become chaos, and I don't want to be around when it all falls apart.

A piercing, explosive ring rises above the murmur of the streets below. It's too late to avoid the chaos, I guess. It wasn't the first gunshot we have heard in the past few weeks. I wonder if that was a shot meant to kill. The thought forces me to close my eyes and exhale completely. I don't know if I could ever justify taking a life.

"Jon," Jo's voice snaps me out of it, "what the hell are we going to do?"

"I'm working on it."

"Well can you clue me in just a little?" Her shortness with me begins. Ever since all of this chaos started we have been getting along.

"We are going to need to get out of here. Apparently some parts of the city have already lost power and water," I respond. Yesterday, when I walked to the hospital, crowds of people in the streets described how parts of the city were deteriorating."

"Let's start thinking of what to do." She pauses, looks down, and then back up to me. "I know the news says we should be okay, but do you think one of us could get sick?"

Her eyes go back to dad's bedroom. The thought of losing him has been thrown to the farthest recesses of my mind.

"I hope not."

Chapter 2: Jonathon

I shut the door and lock it with my sister around my left arm. Dad had passed away in the night and we just finished our goodbyes. We didn't know where to take him. 911 was busy every time we had tried to call in his last few hours. I never imagined feeling so alone in the middle of a city. Outside, the world seems to be getting louder and louder; it is the deafening sound of death striking home after home. When I look down from the sixteenth story of our apartment complex, I see crowds swarming the streets. Our neighbors on either side have remained silent. Either they are dead or have already left the city. I guide my sister to the dining room table, her unfinished cake still before her. As dad became worse and worse, she never left his side and her project remained unfinished. Inhaling, I barely make out the smell of the frosting, still waiting to be decorated.

I walk to the window and press my forehead against the glass. The orange glow of morning lights up the streets and the masses of people below. Cars honk, people yell, and there seem to be a few dead bodies just lying alongside some buildings. No, they must be just resting. How could people just leave someone dead alongside a building? They can't be dead and just lying there. My eyes twitch back and forth. My hand, unbidden, rises to my face to wipe away the tears that I anticipate. But none surface. As I force my hand slowly to my side, I consider why. Maybe I am in shock.

I take my head off the window and turn to see my sister whose head has sagged, supported by her arm stretched across the table. Tears have not abandoned her. We knew this was coming, but it didn't make it any easier. Before my father died, he reached with a finger and beckoned for me to come nearer. I sat on the wooden stool next to his bed and Jocelyn stood at the foot of his bed. It took all his strength as he took a deep breath and began.

"Both of you..." coughs rattled his sentences, "get out of the city. Things are going to get bad out there. Man vs. Man. Get into the country. Take care of each other. It will get better. Until..." he worked his jaw, trying to manage his breath. Dad had given a lot of thought into his final words. "Take the gun, all the essentials here, and the car. Don't stop anywhere. People will get desperate. They won't act like they normally will, even children will change. Humanity will disappear." He seemed to have no life left. He was completely drained and sweat soaked his hair and pillow. Without warning, he reached up grabbed my shirt and pulled me inches from his mouth.

"Don't let me down again."

That last exertion rendered him unconscious. That would be the last thing he ever said to me. For a few moments I hated him for leaving me with that. I have tried so hard to make up for my sins. It never was enough for him. By the time he took in his final breath, that hate turned into understanding. I promised him and myself at that moment, when I pulled the sheet over his face, that I would not mess up again. Not like last time...

"We need to get started," I say to Jo after a long silence, still leaning with my fist against the window. I quickly explain what dad suggested to me in the end. It sounded good enough for me. Better than our idea to try and run for the border. She looks up at me, nodding through the tears.

Before I know it, Jo and I are running about the apartment packing book-bags and the single suitcase we owned. We load the black suitcase with all of the food from the kitchen that would last: canned soup, peanut butter, crackers, a few bottles of water, rice, and some other random assortments we could manage from the already meager cabinets. Our last shopping trip was a week ago and the grocery store was already bare. People were stocking up.

We each gather some clothes. Fall had just begun so we also want to prepare for the winter ahead. We pack everything as tightly as we can and place it by the door. The piece of luggage is heavy but luckily it has some wheels and our backpacks pull tightly against our shoulders. As we stand there, we both glance back at the apartment. I think we both feel the same eerie feeling: we will never see our home again. This was not our first home, in fact we had moved around a lot, but it was our longest home in the past few years since mom died. Beside the television set was a photograph from three years ago, the last one with mom. It was at some picnic. We all look so happy. Dad smiles ear to ear with mom around his left arm and Jo and me under his right. Jo was starting to look a lot like mom. They had the same strawberry blonde hair and wore it nearly the same way. Dad and I didn't look too much alike, but we shared the same eyes. That was one of the last times we would be together as a family. We lost mom a few weeks later. Now, we just lost dad. I feel the tears from earlier creep up on me. I shake my head. Jo seems to have read my mind as she goes to the photograph, takes it out of the frame, and tucks it into her bag.

I almost forgot. There is only one more thing to get.

I finally step over to the closet and bring down my dad's safe box, or whatever you call it. The combination is simple: 888. I look in at its contents, and a small revolver with a half empty box of bullets peers back up. I don't really like guns. I stuff it in my jacket pocket and put the rest of the bullets in my book bag. My sister gives me a weary look.

"You could never use that." she says, worried. And she is right.

"I know," as I fumble with it in my pocket, trying to make it look less noticeable. "It may help with a bluff though. Hey, maybe I could shoot a deer with it when we get settled."

Jocelyn's eyebrow rises. I don't know the first thing about deer hunting. I exhale with a mild grin. It was a poor joke.

"We'll figure it out," she returns with a half smile. A smile of uncertainty. "Let's get going. Dad would have wanted us to leave as soon as we could."

"What should we do with dad?" I ask. Leaving him there didn't seem like the best option. He should be buried. Jo looks at me and her eyes show a struggle with what to do.

"If things get under control we will come back and take care of him. There's no time." She responds. It's not what she wants to do, but it's what we have to do.

I pull the door to the hallway open and slowly step outside as a very reasonable fear settles in. I don't know what to expect out here, and I don't know if I'll be capable of making all the right decisions. This apartment was the last place we had control. Outside-things were completely out of our hands. Jo begins slowly down the hall toward the staircase that leads to the parking garage. There's no time to obsess about the future now; we need to move. Instinctively, I turn and lock the door behind me. Habit, I guess.

We begin our walk slowly down the hall. The hall feels like a passageway to hell. It's quiet except for the muffled noises in the streets echoing through the wall. After going down one flight of stairs, it gets dark.

The power goes out.

It is pitch black aside from the emergency exit sign that leads to the parking garage. We fumble through the dark as I drag the luggage down the steps. I open the door to the garage and my eyes adjust to the light. My nose fills with an awful stench and I try to grab Jo's head to cover her eyes, but I am too late.

Chapter 3: Jocelyn

Bodies. At least half a dozen piled on top of each other beside the entrance to the garage. I could tell that Jon had tried his best to turn my head, but the horrors lock my gaze. Maggots and flies swarm the gray faces as they glare up at me. I turn and taste vomit in my mouth. This is barbaric that someone would leave this here. No one even tried to cover them up. They just lay there. Jon takes my bags and nudges me along. I don't know why, but my legs feel like bricks. It seems they want me to stand there and gaze at these sunken faces. But soon, I move on. I ask for my bags back, but he says not to worry about it. Jon tries to be protective; it makes him feel better.

I wipe my mouth with my arm.

"I'm okay; let's just keep going," I mumble out. I'm really not sure if I am, but I needed to say it. I start to walk quicker, ahead of Jon, to where we parked the car last week. Not many cars are left. A few have shattered windows and the resulting shards of glass crunch beneath my boots. They seem to have been rummaged through and some have their gas tank lids open. I hear the wheels of the luggage as Jon follows me, but they don't come close to drowning out the sound of the people outside. The crowds in the streets seem louder in the garage. I feel so uneasy, thinking about how everything would become so mad, especially when Jon and I have remained so calm throughout this ordeal. I guess we are a minority. We arrive at dad's white SUV and load in what's left of our home. Luckily, unlike most of the cars in the garage, it hasn't been damaged. Jon takes the driver seat. We drive down the gray concrete garage. Jon has to steer around a few cars that look like they've broken down. Our SUV takes us around and around to the exit of the garage. I put on my sunglasses as the early sun blinds my vision at the exit.

I wish I could have remained blind because the streets lie in complete chaos. It's indescribably painful to see my home and my neighbors tearing themselves apart. Storefronts along the tall buildings are shattered open. Bodies line the streets. I see people yelling, just next to some children who are crying without anyone paying them any mind.

"This isn't possible." I mutter to Jon. He brings the car to a stop right outside the parking garage. His bulging eyes and slightly open mouth convey that he's just as shocked.

"My God, this is out of control. It seemed…more contained from so far up. It was not even this bad yesterday. We need to get out of here." As Jon finishes his last words, I see a man point toward us. He must be approaching his twenties. The man's mouth moves, as if to shout to all of those around him. I cannot hear him. At least twenty more eyes peer at us. Most are teenagers.

"Jon, get us out of here. What do they want?"

He turns the car away from the strangers and hits the accelerator. "Probably a running car. Not a lot of people in the city have a car-everyone who did probably left, or at least tried."

Few people dwell in the opposite direction of that soon-to-be mob. I turn around and watch as the crowd of people, my age, slowly drifts away. After I breathe a sigh of relief, Jon and I exchange glances and drive forward. Young children look lost and older ones try to give comfort. Maybe they are headed to hospitals and police stations in search of some help-any help. Some seem to be all alone, and I feel horrible for them. I wish I could help all of them somehow. A few more cars pass us on the left, on the other side of the yellow line. We are all heading out of the city, and I imagine that some of these people don't even know where their ultimate destination is.

Jon slouches down to look at the road signs at the top of the telephone poles. "We need to get to one of the bridges."

Jon pulls up to a red light and the car comes to a halt. There doesn't seem to be any cross-traffic, but why chance it, I guess. There's certainly no reason to stop for fear of the police. As we are stopped, Jon looks over to me.

"We are gonna make it though this, I promise." he fakes a smile. I know he means it, but this madness is far out of either of our control.

"I know." I say back, not making eye contact. I push my hair behind my ear and stare at the red light. Jon leans forward and squints his eyes at me. No, not at me- past me and out the window. I turn my head and see a boy waving; he is maybe 18 or 19. Behind him, there are a few others of his age. He returns Jon's look with a smile and approaches the car. Jon rolls down my window to talk to him. The boy's head is only a few feet from my own.

"Hey, Darry. Man! How have you been making out?" Jon asks, observing Darry's fatigued features. He sounds almost too casual. Our father just died. Most of the city just died. My chest tightens.

"My folks were two of the first to go, right when school was canceled. We have been managing ever since. Good to see you made it out alright." Darry slowly responds. His sunken eyes shift to me then back to Jon. He leans in slightly and looks into the backseat. "Where are you two headed?"

"Out of here. I thought the country may be a better place to wait this one out." Jon answers as I nod in agreement. Dad thought we should get out to the country. Regardless, the plan seems strange to discuss with others. Darry looks to the left and his right then back to Jon.

"That's a good idea. Sorry it's not going to work out." Darry smirks. I am not sure what he means, but then I feel his knife resting against my throat.

Chapter 4: Jonathon

"Sorry to do this to ya Johnny, but I need your car. It's hard enough to find one around here, and then you come rolling up like it's an ordinary Friday night. Get out now, unless you want to watch your sister choke on her blood." Darry says darkly as he presses the blade against Jo's neck.

"Darry, what are you...is this how it is now?" The words stumble from my mouth. Darry's mouth curls and he beckons to the one woman on his left.

"Baby, go open up the driver's door and help him out" Darry barks. Some skinny brunette moves around to the front of the car over to my side. My left hand slips down and hits the door lock. Jo looks over to me, her eyes widen. Her hand trembles in her lap and she shakes her head ever so slightly. She wants to know what I'm doing. I wish I knew. The brunette tries to open my door.

"Darry, he locked it." she whines. She begins to bang on the window with a fist. I look over to Darry. His upper lip twitches.

"Do you wanna see her dead man? Do it now!" He pushes the blade into her neck. A single drop of blood slowly runs down. "I will do it Jon. Please don't test me. I have no choice."

"Alright! Let me get my seat belt." I immediately reach down, but into my coat pocket. The center console hides my hand. I grip the pistol. He doesn't fall for it.

"I wanna see your hands! Unlock your door first." Darry yells, and the blade goes a little deeper. My sister inhales and mouths a silent scream. I freeze.

"Sorry, sorry. I wasn't thinking." The words rush out. My left hand goes toward the unlock button, but my right stays gripped to the handle of the revolver. I can already feel my palm sweating.

"Now," he yells even louder. He curses at me and points the blade at me for a second. Before he can return it to my sister's throat, I draw out the gun between the blade and my sister's head with the barrel lined up perfectly with his forehead. His jaw nearly unhinges and his eyes dilate. His blade falls to the car mats. I tilt my head forward and look at him from the tops of my eyes. I've never felt such concentrated rage.

Darry stutters, frozen. "No man, I wasn't gonna do it. It was all for show."

"Back up!" I command venomously, unsure if my hand is shaking from the rage or the fear. My sister gasps and her hand goes to the cut on her neck. I see the trickle of blood run down her green pea coat. I consider shooting him, and my finger twitches in anticipation. I feel it tighten more and more around the trigger. The hammer begins to pull back...

"Let's just go." Jo yells. That was all I needed. My finger loosens and I put my foot on the accelerator and we drive off down the road. I look in the rear-view mirror and see Darry, the brunette, and the rest of his group standing in the middle of the road.

We take the exit to the bridge and the next ten minutes are completely silent. We reach the other side of the bridge just before the tunnel penetrates a high hill. Surprisingly there is no one around the tunnel's entrance. Some of the cars and crowds must have deterred people trying to find a way out. Both of my hands are shaking. The gun is on the floor next to the knife. I hate guns. My stomach leaps to my mouth so I pull over for a second. I open my door and run around the car to the side of the bridge. The river is far below, but I can hear the sound of the rushing water. It doesn't help calm me down; I vomit.

Reaching into my pocket, I pull out an old receipt and wipe my mouth. It's not the best method, but it cleans me up. I crush it into a ball and throw it below. I don't think the police will be giving me a fine for littering today. I feel a hand on my back.

"You did what you had to do," Jo calmly says.

"It's not what I did. It's what I almost did. I wanted to shoot him. All I wanna do is go back there and put a bullet in his head. He hurt you. He lied to me." I take a few breaths, realizing how much my anger is coming through in my words. "Who else is he now going to hurt?"

"Maybe now he will think twice. And I am okay. It's not deep - it already stopped bleeding." A maroon smudge is all that is left of where Darry cut her. I look at her neck worried. She smiles slightly. "I'll be fine. Trust me."

"I knew things were going to change. I never imagined like this."

"We will be okay." She pats my back, and gives me a slight hug. The first she has given me in a long time. "Let's go."

We both get back in the car. I pick up the gun and return it to my pocket. It had been three years since I held a revolver like that. I notice Jo has the knife in her hands. It's a small switch blade. She wipes her blood off of it and folds it into her pocket. I switch the transmission to drive and we enter the tunnel. Perhaps things are better on the other side.

Chapter 5: Sara

Hunger.

I have never felt so hungry before. Mom and dad would never have allowed it. I miss them even thinking about them. It has been about one week since they died in the hospital. They died nearly minutes apart in two hospital beds right next to each other with my sister and me looking up from their feet. I cried a lot that day. So did my twin sister.

The nurse told us to wait in the room outside. She said she would find someone to take us- to take care of us. As we waited, more and more people were rolled into the room where my parents died. They were all coughing and sweating. My sister and I stayed hand in hand as I watched the clock. The long hand went around and around. The nurse never came back.

Finally, we walked down to the front desk. A woman was behind the counter. She was sweating, too, and looked very tired. More people were rushing into the hospital and many were shouting at her. Everyone seemed so angry. I worked up the courage and shouted, "Excuse me."

She continued to work. I shouted louder. She kept writing on forms and talking to the adults swarming around us. As I felt a tear run down my cheek, our eyes met. She put the phone into her chest and leaned into me. She kinda smelled and looked like she had been playing outside in the hot sun.

"Hey, sweetie," she coughed. I could hear a person on the phone yelling louder. She yelled back in the telephone, "Give me a minute." Her eyes returned to me. Despite all the other people in the room she gave me her complete attention. "Do you two have somewhere you can go?" She coughed more. She sounded really bad.

My sister was still holding on to my hand and I looked up at the nurse. I think she was a nurse, anyway. Using my hand I wiped the tears away and shook my head. I wanted to say "My grandma," but she lived in Michigan with the rest of our family. Daddy had just been given a new job. My sister and I had only gone to one day of fourth grade before mom first got sick. We had no one. The tears began again. The lady looked at us both, and she looked sad. I could tell she wanted to help us, but she couldn't. More people pushed toward the nurse. My sister and I had to hold on to the counter so we would not be pushed away.

She reached onto the counter and grabbed a paper and scribbled a phone number. "This is the number for people who can help you. They are gathering children like you so they can take care of you." She finished and barely smiled at me. Then she resumed her work. I looked at my sister and I could tell she heard everything, too.

"If they are going to take us, I want to get some things from home first." I said.

"I don't know. I think we should leave, Sara. That's what that woman said." my sister responded.

I didn't think she was right at the time and I convinced her to go back home. When we left the hospital, it was completely crazy outside. Cars were backed up and crowds walked all over. Luckily my sister remembered how to get home. Since we lived so close, my parents had walked to the hospital a few days before. I wanted them to take an ambulance then, but they said they were all busy helping more sick people.

We pushed past others that were walking in the streets; some were in such a hurry. One man knocked me down as he passed trying to keep himself up. I watched him fall down a few steps behind us. That really scared me. Luckily, we were able to push through and made it to the apartments. It seemed like it took all day, but finally we were climbing up the stairs to the door.

"Do you have the key mom gave us?" I asked my sister. She looked at me. Her eyes were watering and her head shook.

"I thought you had one." We stood there in silence at the front of our door. That door was the difference between home and the world, and I thought that if we got back inside, we could hide for a little bit more. Now, we don't have that option. Suddenly, all the sadness and fear came upon both of us at the same time. I sat against the door and she sat beside me. We did not blame each other. We just cried and held onto one another. I thought at the time that would be the worst moment of my life. Both of us were lost without anyone, just a stupid phone number we had forgotten about at that point. We fell in and out of sleep. I thought I would never feel so hopeless.

I was wrong.

We woke up the next morning, curled up next to each other. Neither one of us remembered falling asleep. Luckily, the phone number was in my hand on a crumpled piece of paper. We pulled ourselves together, went down to the street, and found a boy that let us use his cell phone. He was like us, but had an older sister who was taking care of him. She didn't want to take care of us too. The people on the other end of the phone told us to try and come to the other side of the yellow bridge. They said they were afraid to bring the bus into the city. She said buses would be going around the city all day and night looking for children like us. I felt a little better then. Maybe we can just escape the city.

They were right about being scared of the city. My sister and I almost didn't make it between all of the angry and sick people as we walked through the streets. We passed many kids that were just sitting and crying. My sister and I promised each other we would be better than that. Sitting and crying was not an option anymore. Finally, after what felt like forever we made it to the end of the yellow bridge that the woman on the phone mentioned. We just waited.

During the first day many cars and groups of people passed us. Now, just one or two come out. I don't think any of them can see us because they just drive past me, even when I wave. No bus has passed by yet.

We have waited for three days.

I peer over the bridge and look back at my sister who is lying on the sidewalk with her dirty and tangled hair strewn around her head. Tear stains on her cheeks show what color her pale skin was before it became brown from the dirt. Her clothes are dirty too, just like mine. Luckily mom and dad had dressed us warm, so when we huddled together the past few nights, we didn't get too cold. We didn't want to miss the bus so we stayed on the dusty street-occasionally taking turns to get drinks from the river.

I sit down on the sidewalk beside my sister. Just as I pull a broken leaf from my sister's hair, a car comes down the bridge. I gave up waving a while back so I just look at it with my eyes. The car slows down!

I think they see us! I shake my sister's head, and just as she looks up, the car pulls over on the other side of the road. A man gets out of the car and walks to the other side of the bridge, leaving his door open. Then I see a girl with beautiful red hair get out and join the man, leaving the car alone. I wish my hair was like that. I do not like how dark it is sometimes.

As they get farther from the car, my heart starts to beat a little faster. I tug on my sister's shirt to get her attention, and we slowly stand up together. I glance back and forth between the car and the man, afraid of what could happen if this doesn't work. With no clear reason, I grab my sister's hand and run softly toward the car.

"What are you doing?" my sister whispers.

"Shh...we will crawl into the back behind the seats. They have to take us. I don't wanna get left." My sister gets into the car and climbs behind the back seat. I start to go in, but then I see a gun. I hesitate, but it's too late, my sister is already in. I follow her and sit behind the back seat. I put my arm over her and we lean our backs against it. We'll be hard to see now.

I hear them get in. My mind is still focused on the gun; it scares me. I hold my sister tighter and put my finger to my lips. She nods at me. I won't let anyone hurt my twin sister, and I know she won't let anyone hurt me.

Everything gets dark as we enter the tunnel.

Chapter 6: Jocelyn

I hope Jon is alright. He will be. He always manages to take care of himself.

I fold the knife and put it in my pocket after wiping the blood off with a rag in the glove compartment. Just wiping it once removed any trace of it from the blade. The knife may come in handy in the future and if my brother has a gun, I at least want a knife. Although, maybe I should take the gun if it's going to keep bothering him. I know it must be difficult for him to even have it in his pocket.

We travel through the tunnel. Occasionally, he swerves around cars that are stopped in the middle. Some have their door open, and some do not. My curiosity asks me to look inside, but I am afraid as to what I may find. More dead?

People who died from the disease, or worse, people who were killed after?

The car begins to approach the other side of the tunnel. More light begins to pour into the car as the entrance gets closer. I look over toward my brother. He has both hands firmly on the wheel and a dead stare locked on the road ahead.

As my eyes adjust I wonder why I am not a mess over this hostage thing, but then I see something that wrenches my attention...

Mud.

It's on the center console, and I don't remember it being there when my brother reached for a gun behind it. And I remember that moment very well. I turn my head toward the backseat. There is nothing there except for a little more mud that seems to drag up on the back of the seat. Those are footprints. Someone is in the car. I glance over to Jon. His eyes are still fixed on the road ahead. He is slowing down since we are about to exit the tunnel. I guess he is afraid of any surprises. I can feel my heart begin to beat through my chest as I look toward the back seat.

Whoever it is must be hiding behind the seat in the cargo space. Someone really quiet, too, if he or she managed to slip in without us noticing at the bridge. Probably someone smart. Maybe someone deadly.

"Jon can we pull over up here, I am not feeling well now." He gives me a frustrated look. The area looks pretty safe. There are only a few vacant cars on the side of the road and some paper flying in the wind. "Please Jon, it's really important." I squeeze his right arm and our eyes meet. His jaw loosens, and his eyes tighten; he now knows something's amiss. He pulls to the side of the road and lets me out. He follows beside me. We both shut the car doors.

"What's wrong?" he whispers as he grabs my shoulders.

"There's someone in the back..." I mumble through my teeth. Instantly, Jon digs back out the gun. I go for the knife and keep my hand in my pocket clutching the handle. We walk slowly around the car, hunched over so that we're below the window line.

"Get behind me." Jon commands, quietly. He prepares the gun in his right hand as he reaches for the trunk handle with his left. He looks at me and mouths, "One, two, three…"

He throws the trunk door into the air and points the gun into the back. Someone huge is hiding back there. Someone filthy. I inhale air in fear. As my eyes focus, I realize that everything I've just thought was wrong, except for the filthy part. It is actually two girls. Both of their blue eyes meet mine. They are quivering. I exhale relief and I feel all my muscles release. I reach to pat Jon's arm down, but he already has the gun dangling toward the ground. He drops it. His right hand shakes.

I study the two girls and how tiny they are. Both had the same blue eyes and dark hair. Maybe it's black but they're both so covered in dirt that I can't tell. They are the most pathetic looking creatures I have ever seen, apparently homeless and hungry, with sunken cheeks and cracked lips. They must be twins. I feel awful. How many other children already look like this?

One of them finally breaks the silence, talking quickly, just like a little girl might if she knows she's in trouble with her parents.

"Please help us, we have no one. We didn't wanna scare you, but we didn't know what to do. We are sorry. We didn't want you to leave us too!" I guess they are around ten or eleven years old. Jon looks at me; his eyebrows show more concern than I normally see on his face. The right side of his face smiles.

It isn't long before Jon is giving the girls as much of our food as they can eat. One is making peanut butter crackers while the other washes down her granola bar with some bottled water. Their faces glow with happiness as they fill their stomachs. We all sit in a circle on the side of the road with some food in between us. I keep anxiously looking around us but it seems to be a pretty safe spot. The one girl offers me my own cracker with her dirty hands. Normally I would want my hand sanitizer, but I eat it anyway, and it tastes even better in front of their smiling faces. I hear a crunch to my left as Jon bites into two crackers on either side of his mouth, making a goofy face that pulls a bunch of giggles from the twins. I sigh again, this time with a little bit of happiness.

Still with a smile on his face, Jon clears his throat after swallowing the crackers and wiping his hands on his jeans. "So now that we've given you half of our food, what are your names?"

"I'm Sara."

"And I'm Caitlyn."

Hearing their lighthearted voices distracts me for just a split second, and I realize that I've already forgotten which is which. "Jon, this is going to be difficult…"

A warm laugh comes from my left as both of us look from one identical face to another. "Yes, yes it will Jo."

No matter how close I look, I can't find an obvious physical difference between the two. Sara tells me their story as Caitlyn continues to eat. Sara seems to be the more outgoing of the two. We sit for another ten minutes and eventually Jon picks up the food. The girls look so sad and stare at him longingly.

"You can't eat much more or you will both get sick." he says through a laugh. "Don't worry we will keep you full of food."

They both smile at him. I had never seen Jon so good with children before, especially considering what I remember when I was younger. I don't know how much longer we will be with these girls, but they quickly brought him a serenity I have not seen in a long time. I smile as the two follow him to the car and pile in the backseat as he finishes putting the food in the trunk.

He looks over at me with a grin, "Looks like you can sit with them." I chuckle in response and nod. He makes his way to the driver's side door, intentionally stepping over the gun still lying on the pavement.

I pick up the gun. He wants me to have it now.

Chapter 7: Jocelyn

As I sit with the twins in the backseat, I remark how quickly they've warmed up to me. It isn't long before the one has her head resting on the side of my arm. They both look exhausted. They are still awake, but their eyelids are fluttering. I put one arm around each of them. The one to my right, maybe Caitlyn, looks up at me with a gentle smile. It soon fades from her face and she falls asleep. The other one follows right behind her.

The car pulls up to a red light and I look out both windows. The streets are still empty. We had passed a car or two and seen the occasional movement behind houses, but things are generally quiet out of the city. I reach up to the wound on my neck, careful not to wake the twin on my right.

The cut reminds me how careful we have to be. Jon turns around to me speaking quietly.

"Well this has changed things."

"Yea, I mean, how much harder is this going to be now? But we can't leave them."

"I never even considered that," he whispers. He changes the subject. We both knew they were staying. "So we still want to head to the ole' campground?"

"Yea that sounds like the best choice. Maybe we should think about stopping and getting some more food– especially with these girls with us now."

"Yea. There's a supermarket on the way there. We should be there in fifteen." Jon puts his foot down and our car continues on the path.

While we were still in the apartment Jon and I talked about what we would do as we packed. With every adult dying, it would not take long for the power and water to go out. Waste wouldn't be collected and people would scavenge for food in the worst of ways. Jon came up with the idea to go to an old campground from our weekend family vacations. It had a water pump, cabins, and electricity (as long as it lasts). Our plan gave us comfort. It gave us hope. It still does, but all the chaos has really dampened our idea of simply living a few weeks camping until the country pulled itself back together. I am afraid that a few weeks could be much, much longer.

I look at each girl and then continue to stare out the window. The buildings of the city are replaced with trees on both sides. I think I like the trees more. The car comes to an intersection and Jon turns. Then, up ahead, I can see the supermarket at the corner-and a car coming straight down our side of the road.

My heart sinks as a red blur bolts toward our car. Jon swears and begins to pull off the road. The red car seems to see us and gets in the correct lane and races past us. They almost killed us. Why weren't they paying attention?

Then I see it. I tell Jon we need to turn around, too.

Now.

Chapter 8: Jonathon

I move my head close to the windshield and squint. Slowing the car, I try to make out the chaos up ahead. My sister yells something, I don't know what exactly; although the hundreds of young people up ahead may have something to do with it.

The supermarket is a beehive. The windows in the front are shattered and the hungry were hopping over them. It looks like a riot on TV. I bring the car to a stop at the entrance to the parking lot. Other cars fly past us out of the exit. A few groups of people carry bags of food and bottles of water. Some are running. Some are bleeding.

I finally get to the point where I can pick out individuals instead of observing just a mob. Most of them are Jo's or my age. I see a few children crying off to one side of the entrance and some people fighting directly in front of them. A body lies on the ground– dead. In the middle of the fight before the door, a single boy emerges, yelling. He raises his arm, and fires a handgun into the air. The piercing sound of the gunshot doesn't seem to surprise anyone other than us. The looting just continues. I feel a hand on my shoulder and my heart jumps to my throat. It is one of the twins: Sara. She speaks softly, her eyes gazing at the crowd.

"Are they all fighting for food?" she asks nervously.

"Yes," I respond. They're doing more than fighting; they're dying for food. I don't know what to say. Another gunshot rings through the buzzing air.

I throw the car in reverse and before I know it I am flying away from the mass of people. My father's warning echoed in my ear. That could have ended worse. I should have listened. The rear-view mirror shows Jo soothing both of the twins by running her fingers gently through their hair. Our eyes meet in the mirror and she mouths, "Let's just get there." I couldn't agree with her more. I nod and we take off down the road, wondering how long it took for the supermarket to go from busy to a complete riot.

The campground is far removed from the city, but it doesn't take too much longer for us to get there. That market sits on the outskirts of town, so the rest of the drive is primarily highway. Some daylight still remains as we approach the park entrance.

As we pull into the campground, it seems empty. A steel gate blocks the access road and I see the lock hanging from the chain binding the gate's entrance. Going around it isn't an option because of the deep ditches and densely packed trees on either side of the road. The ranger station is just beyond this obstacle. The key should be inside.

"I'm going to go see if there's a key," I quietly say to Jo and the girls. "Stay here; I won't be long."

The sun is going down and the trees cast eerie long shadows against the station's walls. I walk up the steps and knock on the fading burgundy door of the silver trailer.

No answer. I knock louder. "Hello, is there anyone in there?" I shout into the trailer as I turn the doorknob. The light on the porch projects into the dark room. It seems empty. I feel the wall for a switch. My hand finds the toggle and the lights come on. It's relieving to know the power was still on in some places. Nothing. The room is empty.

I exhale a sigh of relief. Then, I feel a hand grab my ankle.

Chapter 9: Jonathon

A scream exits my mouth for the first time in years. I look straight down and see a man sprawled out on the floor. One hand is around my leg and the other is stretched out beside him. The floor around him is smeared with blood. The man looks up at me, his face swollen with a blistering rash covering its side. This is the worst case of the infection I have ever seen, and it's the most horrified I've ever felt. I can't help but silently pray that I will never end up on the ground gasping for air and soaking in my own blood.

My fears are interrupted by a pleading groan from the ranger. His bloodshot eyes look up at me, and they beg for help.

I feel bad that I screamed.

Without much hesitation, I bend down turn him over and carry him into the main room. He is very light and his ranger uniform is noticeably loose; there is almost nothing to him. I set him down delicately on the couch. As I pull away, I pause at the blood stains that are now on my own clothes. He looks up at me with grateful eyes and manages a small smile. I guess he is around forty years old, but now he seems more like a helpless child. I notice his right hand hanging over the side is shaking. A blanket rests on the chair beside him and I throw it over him. His eyes again show thanks. I can tell he is trying to speak, but he fails and quickly gives up.

The door to the trailer flies open. My sister walks in with the gun at the ready. She heard my scream. It only takes a second for her to see the ranger. She immediately looks at me, her eyebrows show an immediate empathy. She kneels beside him, at a lost for words.

Then she musters up the courage and delicately says, "What can we do?" His bloodshot eyes stare back into hers. His chest expands as he gasps for air. After a moment, he changes his gaze to the kitchen.

"Medicine? Painkillers? Water?" Jo questions the man. He manages to shake his head just a little. Jo looks back at me. "Go to the kitchen and see if you can find anything."

There are no decorations, and the only appliances are a tiny stove and a fridge. Between them is a table big enough for one. On the table is a vinyl tablecloth and a handwritten note sits on top of that. That won't help him.

"Ask him if it's in a cabinet or something." I start to open drawers. I hear Jo speaking to him, but I don't hear a response. I go through drawer after drawer and find nothing aside from some aspirin. The fridge has some food but nothing helpful. I walk back over and kneel beside my sister.

"There isn't anything I can find. What do you need?" I calmly ask. I want to help him more than anything. Again, his eyes go to the kitchen then back to mine. Then his eyes drop to his hand. With his hand he presses two fingers together with his thumb and slowly moves it back and forth. I begin to run through all the things he could be doing. What does he...a pencil. He is writing. I look around the room for a second. Maybe a prescription. Then I remember the note.

"The note?" I curiously ask. He nods a fraction of an inch. I hurry to grab the note and bring it back to him. He sees it and nods again. I hold it out so my sister can also see it, and we both begin reading.

Chapter 10: William

Never before have I experienced pain like I bear now. It has been nearly a week since I first showed the signs and somehow I have managed this long. It began when I noticed my chest was a bright red color in the mirror. Then the rest of the horrors followed. However, none of the pain I physically dealt with prepared me for what was to come.

It was the day after I had become ill that I saw my wife succumb to the same illness. When I first saw the rash on her back, I walked into the bathroom and cried my eyes out. The disease at that point was all over the country. I thought we could avoid it if we secluded ourselves at the ranger station in the woods.

I was wrong. It infected me and she refused to leave.

A month ago, I had held my wife's hand as she fought against cancer. Those tears and long nights seemed to be worth every minute when the doctor told us that it had gone into remission. I had never felt so happy as we held each other in tears of joy. It seemed we had managed through better or worse. Things became much worse. A month after her remission, we were in the middle of the woods trying to fight another disease. It all seemed futile.

The plague was much harder on her. She was bedridden that night and needed to rest constantly. I think it was my love to take care of her that helped me to hold on so long while fighting my own symptoms. She died the following night in my arms as I sat in bed. I prayed that I would just die at that moment too, but I knew I wasn't going to get any breaks. I kissed her forehead.

The virus had quickly changed her face, but she was still beautiful to me.

I wanted to take care of her body properly. I took a shovel from the shed and I buried her behind the station. The sores became worse and each time I drove the spade into the earth-I ripped more skin open. After lashing together two pathetic looking crosses the job was finished despite the debilitating pain. I carried her in, buried her, and read what prayers I could remember from church. I doubted God was listening, but it is what she would have wanted. Then I stuck in the one cross. The other, I hoped would be mine one day- right beside her. When I finished I realized how exhausted I was. My shirt stuck to my body with sweat and blood. I fell to my knees twice on the way to the ranger station alone. I didn't have anything left in me.

I walked to the bathroom, stripped, and turned the shower on. I tried to remain standing, but it was not to be. My knees fell to the floor, and they stayed there. The water turned pink as it washed off my body. I was in pain all over. The campground relied on a ground water source and should keep running for a long time. I stumbled out of the bathroom and changed into my uniform- the last clean clothes. In the kitchen, I tried to eat some food, but I threw it back up into the sink. The only thing that I could manage was a few sips of water. I fell into a chair at the table. A tablet and pen rested on it from when my wife and I planned to make a shopping list just a few days before. I saw her handwriting. Milk, marshmallows, strawberries... It was too much; sobs erupted uncontrolled from my throat. Each item brought up the simplest of memories that

I couldn't repress. I told her I didn't need my lactose intolerance pills as I ate a bowl of cereal. I was up that entire night, and she never said I told you so. I once had teased her about how terrible she was at roasting marshmallows, as I pulled my own pathetic, sticky, black blob on a stick out of the fire pit. The sweet strawberries were her favorite on the hottest of days and blackest of nights.

Dots of salt water consume the paper until I finally muster the strength and courage to grasp the pen. I didn't know who I was writing to, but I need someone to talk to. Even if it is only a piece of paper.

"To whoever finds this-

I don't have long left. Burying my beloved wife robbed me of the last strength I had. She lies behind this ranger station. I am sure you can find the place beneath the soft soil. We tried our best to hide from death, but we were not so fortunate as to escape its wrath. My time is short. If one of the poor children left behind should find this note soon, throughout this station you will find food and water that my wife and I hoped would sustain us. Now I hope it may sustain you in your time of need. There is a safe in the back with a rifle. These woods are full of game, and if the virus has not spread to animals, you should be able to survive for a long time on the campground."

I glance over my writing. It slowly becomes harder and harder to read. My hands are shaking; my vision blurs worse. I am thirsty. I am cold. I scribble a few more words, the combination to the safe, and lay it on the table. My legs carry me, barely, to the main room. They feel like rubber, and my entire body aches. Every breath burns my insides. I support myself from the couch then to the wall but my own weight becomes too much for me. I slide down the wall to my knees. The lights turn off; I must have hit the switch. I struggle my left arm up the wall, but I cannot find it. The little air in my lungs bursts through my mouth as I fall forward onto my chest. The bathroom is just a few feet away. I want to crawl in the shower and turn on the water so bad. I can feel my shirt again sticking to the blood slowly oozing from the sores all over me again.

I can't crawl. I can't yell. My body shuts down. I give up and close my eyes. Maybe someone will find this station. I'll be dead, but maybe, just maybe, I will have helped them.

Chapter 11: Jocelyn

Jon and I finish the note, and he sets it on the coffee table. Many of the strokes had been unintelligible, and I don't think either one of us have the heart to try to interpret them. I look up into the ranger's eyes. His pain seems to be gone. A small smile hides in the corners of his lips. I don't know how much stuff he left us, but it may save all of our lives. I bring my hand to his hair and rub my thumb on his forehead. His hair is sticky. I whisper, "Thank you." The smile leaves his face. His eyes close and his body finally gives out. Jon is standing next to me, and he squeezes my shoulder delicately before reaching for the blanket. He clasps the edge and pulls the cover gently over the man's peaceful face.

* * *

After a few moments I stick my head out to check on the girls. Both of them are in the passenger seat with their eyes locked on the door. I should have told them everything was okay a while ago. My brother has already begun to search the trailer, so I catch up. We find more food, gallons of fresh water, and some tools including an ax, saw, and shovel. The two of us manage to stuff everything in the trunk of the car along with a first aid kit attached to the front of the trailer. We make our final trip through the ranger's home. I was to get the rifle, and Jon needed to find the key to the gate.

"It's so quiet…" I whisper to myself. The crickets don't even seem to feel like talking right now. Carefully turning the dial on the gun safe breaks the silence. He has an assortment of guns. A rifle, shotgun, and several boxes of bullets are all inside. I stuff the boxes in my pack and sling the guns over my shoulder. These will definitely come in handy.

As I walk out of the bedroom I see Jon shaking the key. "It was in a nail on the wall," he says. His eyes turn to the man on the couch. "I will come back tomorrow and bury his body- next to his wife."

"We all will come back." I reply.

"No," he snaps back. "Sorry, I want to do it myself. I can't explain it." I was in no mood to question him now; I would in the morning.

We shut the lights off and I join the girls in the backseat. The least bit of dust is kicked up behind Jon as he walks purposefully to the gate, key in hand. He jogs back as soon as the lock is open, and we drive through. Not too long after we pass, he slams on the brakes and puts it in park. I give him an odd look. He swings open the door and walks back to the gate. I begin to open my door to yell at him. However, I see him shutting the gate and locking it. He returns to the car and we continue to the cabin.

"After all I've seen today, I'm not letting anyone else easily get up here." he says. I nod my head. I couldn't agree more.

Although the cabin was in the same park, it was a long way from the ranger's station. In the darkness Jon struggles to keep the car on the road. The tiny eyes of raccoons reflect the headlights at every turn as our SUV descends further into the forest. When we find the cabin, Jon parks well off of the dirt road and as close to the cabin as possible. It's been a long time since I've been here, but it still looks the same: unaffected by time.

Jon uses the ranger's keys to open the front door. Both of the girls are right behind me as I shine the flashlight through the cabin. He flips the light switch and the whole cabin is illuminated. The place does have everything we will need: four bunk beds lined against the far left wall, a wooden stove in the middle against the back wall, a closed off area to the right with bathrooms, and a shower.

"Please let there be hot water..." I say hopefully.

For now this place would suffice. We unpack everything throughout the cabin. The girls help Jon and me bring everything into the kitchen area against the back wall, and we fill what appears to be some sort of pantry. I begin to sort it all out as Jon grabs the last few things from the car. I hear the car lock, and Jon returns, locking the front door behind him. I look up at him and we both nod.

We made it.

Both girls sit on one of the benches, looking at me. Which one is which is still beyond me. "Well, girls, what do you say we get you both cleaned up?" They return with smiles. Sara, or is it Caitlyn, still has broken leaves throughout her hair.

Jon tosses two towels from our bags and a plastic bag filled with soap and shampoo. I check the bathroom and the girls head in. Some steam pours out from under the door shortly after they've turned on the shower. Another victory. Within fifteen minutes, the girls are already out and dressed in some of my clothes that barely fit them. They look completely different now. Their skin is almost white and their hair is nearly black-it makes their eyes seem almost neon blue. They start to do each others' hair into long pigtails. I let them be.

Behind me, Jon continues sorting through everything. He yawns, clearly exhausted by the events of the day.

"Some of this can wait." I reassure him.

"I know; I'm almost done. It's been a long day." he answers. His eyes look heavy.

"I'm going take a shower and then go to bed. I need to rinse this day off," I say to him after I feel that both girls are situated. He nods and I grab my things for the bathroom.

I shut the wooden door. My entire body feels exhausted, and I strip to nothing and stand in front of the shower head. My bare feet shuffle through the warm puddles left over from the twins' showers. The water is ice cold, but it does not even phase me – I guess they used all the hot water for one night. I close my eyes and let the water run down my face. I start to think of the entire day: Dad, the bodies, the knife, the girls, the supermarket, the ranger. I feel so overwhelmed that I brace myself against the wall with my pruning hand. My heart begins to beat faster and I feel the mask that I've worn all day finally give out. I crouch down and bring my knees to my chest. The tears running down my face feel no different than the water. This cannot be reality. All of this chaos, death, and responsibility. I cannot do this.

I pinch the undersides of my arms. Please wake up, please wake up, please wake up.

Chapter 12: Jonathon

"I hope you two love chicken noodle soup." I yell to the girls as I set another can at that end of the table. Between the ranger and our house we have thirteen huge cans already of that alone. They only complain a little. I think they understand. The stacks of cans and bottled water grow as I empty the ranger's boxes out. The more I organize the more I start to see the bigger picture and it scares me. Before this moment, I have only concentrated on getting us here; now here we are. I don't know how to begin sustaining us in the woods. I have sorted through most of the supplies, but I know they won't last. I need to provide for the four of us, and I need to learn how to do it yesterday. I knew this responsibility would fall on me but it's beginning to hit home as I place another pack of rice amongst the others.

"Damn…" I whisper, realizing how little I knew about hunting or gardening or farming or surviving. Being tired doesn't help all the questions that have flooded my mind. I began sorting through our circumstances: What if we have to leave? Is anywhere completely safe? What's happening out there? How can I possibly know what to do if I don't know what's happening? How can I protect the girls? Exactly how much danger are we facing? Why is this happening?

"Jon?" a soft and quavering voice floats across the room from the bed-side wall. I look over to see a frightened look on Sara's face as she sits up. Somewhere in the past few minutes I had sat down on an old stool, and I guess I've barely moved. My hand clenches in a trembling fist around a can of sweet potatoes. As I blink, I notice how dry my eyes are: probably from letting my eyes bulge for that amount of time.

"I'm sorry Sara," I say finally, exhaling. My expression changes to a smile, "I just can't stand sweet potatoes. Have you decided where you're sleeping? We have a lot of choices…"

"My sister will take this bottom bunk. The top bunk's a little scary for her right now."

"I was never a fan of heights, myself." I fib to Caitlyn.

Caitlyn nods quickly, kicking her feet as her legs hang from the side of one of the other beds. Her hands are folded, and she, too, looks sleepy.

"Go to sleep girls. We are safe out here." It feels good to say that, even though I haven't the slightest clue what the rest of the night has in store for us. I seem to have said it convincingly though. Sara is already nimbly climbing the ladder to get to the top bunk. She is definitely the more outgoing of the two. Through the entire duration of this ordeal, Caitlyn has just stayed in her shell. I can't really blame her. If I don't know what to make of it, how can I expect an eleven year old girl to?

"Good night, you two." They are both asleep within a few moments.

The brief conversation was a pleasant distraction from the swarm of questions that had paralyzed me earlier. I sit on the nearest bunk and lie down for a second and interlock my fingers behind my head. I have so many questions running through my mind. How can I expect to sleep tonight?

Food, shelter, clothing. We have all of these things right now. What do we need that we don't have? Medicine. If one of us does get sick, the best that we have to offer right now is water and blankets. I'll find a way to be ready. I do need to go bury the ranger tomorrow. Maybe there are still more supplies in the trailer that I can bring back. Food, clothing, shelter, medicine. The only other thing I can think of right now is weapons, and we have a few of those. Not that any of us know how to really use them.

Jo comes out dressed to sleep. A towel is wrapped around her hair and she's rubbing it with her hands. Her eyes are almost as red as the few strands of hair that fall across her face. Droplets of water fall to the floor as she stops in front of me. Several times, she inhales deeply and exhales quickly, clearly wanting to say something each time but not finding any words.

"We're going to be alright. We have everything we need to take the time to figure it all out," I say, more convincingly than I had hoped. Jo's eyes shut, and after a brief pause, she nods.

The other bed rustles as Jo climbs in.

It feels like only a moment has passed, but deep down I know that it's been much longer. Maybe more than an hour. I won't let them down. Nobody should be able to make it out here for a while anyway, if ever.

"Don't let me down again…" Those words run through my head on loop, echoing through my mind. Eventually, sleep breaks through and takes me.

Chapter 13: Sara

A creak. It can't be the wind; there are no other creaks to go with it. There is no whistle, not even the sound of the trees. My eyes dart around the room, but it's so dark. I remember Jocelyn went to sleep on the bottom bunk of the other bed, and Caitlyn is below me, but I don't know where Jon is. Please be him, please be him…

Another creak. It's coming from the front of the cabin. Why would Jon be sneaking this late? Maybe he doesn't want to wake us. My chest feels tight and I feel like screaming, but I don't know what will happen. The more I try to listen the more I hear my heart beating: faster and faster.

Another creak, longer this time, but it's different. The front door is opening! The outline of a man becomes clear, but he's leaving! It's not Jon; Jon isn't that tall. What does he have in his hand?

I can't hold it in. I try so hard, but I can't do it. A little whimper escapes me and the man turns with a start, looking right at me. There's no way he can see me. It's too dark! Please don't see me. Trembling, I look at the shadowy man. I won't even breathe. Even if I wanted to, I don't think I could. Just leave!

Almost as abruptly as he had looked at me, the man darts out the door, silently. I won't move, not yet. He needs to be far away. My heart is still beating so loudly that I can't hear anything else.

Just another moment, and then I'll climb down. I need to find out what he was doing. I slowly pull my blanket back with my right hand. A flashlight is in my left hand. I pull it back so slowly so that when I'm uncovered, enough time will have passed. It's so hard to climb off the top bunk.

My legs swing over the head rail, and I find the rungs. They're cold and damp. It feels like the room is foggy. Three more rungs. It's hard to climb while holding something. Two more rungs. Why are they wet? And why is it so cold? I can't slip! I'll make too much noise. He might still be close enough to hear. One more rung. I extend with my right arm as much as I can so I can lower my foot to the ground.

But it doesn't reach the ground. It stops short on something, and slips. I let out a squeal as my hand falls off the bed rail. I fall onto this thing in a total panic. I can't even think. I stand up as quickly as I can and turn on the flashlight.

All I can do now is scream, and it echoes through the whole cabin. I had landed on the body of the nurse from the hospital. I try to turn away but there are just more of the people from the hospital on the floor, lying there. I don't remember inhaling, but I scream again, and I keep screaming. Why is nobody waking up? Where is Jon? Where is Jocelyn? Where is Caitlyn?

I hear a slam and I wheel around just in time to see the outline of the man in the open door frame.

"Wake up!" I hear him yell, but it sounds like Jon. He's too big to be Jon!

"Wake up!" I blink and the door frame turns into the ceiling. Jon is leaning over me with a flashlight in one hand and my shoulder in the other. As I sit up, panting, I start to understand that I was dreaming, but the screams were real.

Caitlyn is in the middle of the room, scared, looking at me with her hands clasped at her chest.

"I'm sorry…"

"It's okay, you're okay." I look over to Jocelyn. She's sitting up on the other top bunk, and she has a soft smile on her face. My breathing slows down almost immediately, but all I manage is a nod and a long gulp to try to relax. Scanning the room, I see that little else has changed from a few hours before. The windows let in a fraction of the morning light. I hope we can all go back to sleep; everyone still looks so tired.

"Do we have to get up now?" I ask.

"No, sleep as long as you need," says Jon, "You're safe here. Try to relax." He lies back down in his bunk and Jocelyn returns to hers. A few minutes go by and I try to shut my eyes. I can't sleep.

The bed starts rocking back and forth, so I peek over the head rail. Caitlyn is climbing up, fumbling on the ladder a little in the dark.

"What are you doing?" I whisper.

"Coming up to see you. I… I wanna see what the top bunk is like." she said with a smile on her face. She sits down at the foot of my bed. I can see the fear in her eyes as she peers over the edge. Her smile becomes uncertain for a moment.

"You're a bad liar; this is too high for you!"

"I am not, and it is not," she argues. I let out a little giggle at that. She grabs my pillow and puts it in her lap. She pats it with her hand. "Now lie down."

"What?"

"Lie down. I wanna play with your hair." she says calmly, like how mom used to say it. There were many times we couldn't fall asleep at home and she would stroke our hair. Before we knew it we were asleep in her lap. I lie down on my side looking at the front door.

"But I'm not tired." I whisper.

"That's okay." she says as she gently separates a handful of my hair between her fingers. I close my eyes for a second and imagine I am with my mom at our old house. Dad is sitting in his recliner with a paper and Caitlyn is fidgeting in his lap with one of her books. It seems like that was just a few days ago. I feel some tears gather in my eyes. Maybe if I try hard enough, this is what I will dream about.

Chapter 14: Caitlyn

I stretch like a cat across the bed as I wake up. Light comes in through the windows of the cabin. Sitting up slowly, I try to remember how I got back to the lower bunk. Sara had fallen asleep while I was playing with her hair, and I had kept going for a while anyway before climbing down. The top bunk didn't seem so bad anymore. Jon is awake, lounging on the bottom of the other bunks. Jo is still asleep on top. Yesterday was long for me so I can't imagine how they feel. I get up and tip-toe to the table, but the creaky floor is annoyingly loud.

"What can we do today?" I say softly out loud, spinning around and forcing a smile on my face. We all slept inside last night, which should make them happy. Those two nights on the sidewalk were awful. Sara stirs, but quickly settles and lays back down, facing the wall. Jon opens his eyes, rolls his shoulders back, and looks at me. It seems like only the bottom half of his face is smiling.

"I guess you are all energized. Are you hungry, Caitlyn? I'm sure I can manage something for our first meal."

I nod a few times, keeping the forced smile on my face. Breakfast has always been my favorite meal. Sara and I didn't have to get cleaned up, or change out of our pajamas. We just threw our covers back and walked to the table. The smell of bacon and pancakes always helped. Mommy and daddy make, or made, the best breakfasts.

My smile stops, and I don't inhale for a little. I watch Jon walk toward the big cabinets next to the stove on the back wall. As he opens the door, a few cans fall from the shelves and hit the wooden floor. The sound is really loud. He quickly turns to me.

"Who packed this?" he asks. I roll my eyes.

Sara stirs a little bit at the sound. She rolls over and opens her eyes.

"Sleep better?" asks Jo, now sitting up. She reaches over and runs her fingers through Sara's hair. Sara nods and my sister and I share a smile.

I feel my eyebrows rise. Thinking of mom and dad took away my appetite. I think I had forgotten when I first woke up. "I take it back. I'm not hungry."

"I know; I don't think any of us are." says Jo, turning toward me but not lifting her hand from Sara's head. "But you have to eat."

I don't say anything back. My head just sinks and my eyes fall to the floor.

"I know things are kinda rough, but they will change," says Jo, quietly. She stands up, hops off the bunk, and walks over to me. I feel her hand under my chin, so I look up to see her kneeling in front of me. That same bottom-face smile that Jon had is on her face, too.

"I really miss my dad too," she says. "But he wanted me to get through this. So I'm going to have to do some things that feel hard for a while. Can you do them with me? Besides we have quite an adventure ahead of us. Also best yet: there will be no school."

"No reading?" Sara nearly falls off her bunk. Jon lifts his head from his search for food.

"Oh no, young lady. You're not going to give up learning on my watch," Jon says with a laugh. I'm not sure if he's serious, but Sara thinks he is, and she is not amused.

"Anyway, Jo's right," he continued, setting some things on the table. "We all have an adventure on our hands. This first one's easy though! We have to eat, and you can choose whatever you like." He throws four unopened bags of mini-muffins on the table. "As long as it's muffins"

"What kind of muffins?" Sara pipes up.

"For your dining pleasure, we have blueberry and banana nut." Jon answers. I remember dad getting them out of a vending machine once for me.

"You're a nut." Jo jokes as she slightly slaps the back of Jon's head. Jon flinches and raises his hand to the spot that she hit, and playfully throws one of the bags of muffins at her.

She catches it just before it hits her in the nose. "Now Jon, don't throw your food." We all laugh.

Sara reaches for a bag, tears it open, and nibbles at a muffin. She never cared for them. Mom's were the only ones she ate.

"Come on over, Caitlyn," says Jon, patting beside himself on the bench.

I don't want muffins. I don't want anything. Jon just continues to look at me as I shake my head.

"How good are they?" asks Jo, looking toward Sara at the table.

Sara doesn't say anything. She doesn't even change her facial expression. She just turns toward Jo and nods with an entire muffin in her mouth. She goes to say something and it almost falls out.

"See? They're good," says Jo. Soon enough, we're all chewing away, except for my sister who is chewing loudly. I hate it when she does that. Daddy would never let her get away with it. Jon passes out some glasses with bottled water poured in them. I drink it down.

Jon crinkles up all the empty bags and sighs. I bet he wishes there are more we could eat today. "I promise breakfast will be a little more creative in the future. I'm going to get back to the trailer. It shouldn't take too long. Plus, I'll see if I can gather anything else from inside."

The smile fades from his face quickly. I'm going to be twelve years old soon, so I can tell when someone is faking. Sara hops off of my bench and runs over to him as he turns around to walk to the door, and I follow. He jumps a little bit as I wrap my arms around his waist.

"Come back soon!" Sara says, doing the same.

This time, his whole face smiles, even if it is just a little one. As he turns away, I feel an odd tingling in my throat and clear it quietly.

Chapter 15: Jonathon

It's hard to leave the girls. I already feel some sense of responsibility for the twins, a need to protect them. Plus, they are one of the few elements of my life that might make me smile anymore. Jo and I have gotten along well these past few days, but once things return to any sense of normalcy our problems will return. The door subtly creaks behind me as I pull it shut, and the storm door slams against the frame as I walk to the car. With a turn of the key, the SUV comes to life and drifts forward from my prompting. Maybe the long drive will give me time to understand why I feel so compelled to bury this ranger.

With nobody else in the car, I'm a little less careful with the drive. It feels good to take the turns a few miles an hour faster than I should: like an amusement park ride. I give the steering wheel a particularly aggressive twist to the left, and the car turns just barely faster than traction should allow. The extra floating dust in my rear-view mirrors confirms the fishtail.

Alright, that's enough goofing off. I need to remain in the right mindset if I'm going to keep everyone safe. No mess-ups. Not now, when there is no telling what the consequences could be. My driving becomes immediately smoother.

As the road flies below me, I turn my attention back to the ranger. I had originally felt a sense of duty or something to this man who had given us supplies that may save our lives as we get used to "living off of the land." The more I think about it, the more I realize that it must be more than gratitude. I understand why I couldn't explain it to Jo yesterday; I can't even explain it to myself.

Maybe since I can't bury my father...

I glance at the radio several times and begin to seek through the stations. Each one is in static. We really are secluded here in the woods. Or maybe they stopped broadcasting. Who would be broadcasting anymore anyway?

The road is becoming less dusty, and I can see pavement up ahead. The ranger's station should be just over this hill. The sun is well into the sky now, and although the warmth is currently pleasing, it might get annoying when I'm trying to dig a grave. Is six feet a requirement or a suggestion? I don't have a clue. It doesn't really matter how deep it is. The grave will be up to my chest. That'll work.

The station is quiet. Undoubtedly much like the rest of campground: an odd sense of stillness. I throw the transmission into park and kill the engine. As I open the door, I hear the sound of birds chirping in the treetops. What would normally have been a serene string of tweeting was unsettling as it was at odds with the rest of the eeriness of the place. I shake my head to get focused. I need a shovel, and I need to find a place to dig.

Both present themselves immediately. On the side of the station, there is an array of tools hanging from a row of nails embedded in the trailer's outside wall. Spades, shovels, rakes, hoes, hand tillers, and even a pitchfork are hung in no immediately apparent particular order. Wait...

Alphabetical? I muse, seeing that the cultivator is first and the watering pot is last. I continue, seeing that a compound bow and quiver is just a few nails to the left of the watering pot. An odd thing to just have lying around. It's been a couple of months since I've shot, but you don't lose something like that very quickly. Archery is more like riding a bike than swinging a golf club. I joined the school's club the past year and was a pretty good shot. I was saving up to by a bow this year. Looks like I will take this one for free.

Again, I need to focus. The place to dig the grave is clear as well. Behind the trailer are two wooden crosses sticking out of the ground. One has a small mound in front of it. The other is at the head of undisturbed soil. A chill shoots through my spine as I consider what it must have felt like for the ranger to lash a cross and hope that it would be over his final resting place.

I make my way into the trailer. The ranger lies on the couch, undisturbed. Only a few flies have found their way into the trailer, and they don't appear to have decided where they want to land. I stop to observe the situation. Wrapped entirely in the blanket, he is just as easy to lift today as he was last night. I navigate carefully out the front door, around the trailer, and I lay him a few feet away from what will be his grave.

I reposition the ranger beside the cross marked patch of dirt and mark the edges of the grave. After hanging the spade back on the wall and trading it for a long, wide shovel, I come back to study the ground.

"Here goes," I say, exhaling heavily through the words.

I was right about the sun. A few dozen shovel-fulls in and I feel the unrelenting heat saturating my back. It was unusually hot for this time of year. All those bodies in the streets – the parking garage, I can only imagine the reek that surrounds them now. Again, I am thankful for getting out of the city.

Time and time again, I stand, empty the shovel, and squat back down for another. Time goes by slowly, but eventually I can tell that the sun is no longer rising higher into the sky. At about the same moment, I start to measure the depth by leaning up against the hole's walls. The hole is a bowl at the moment, so soon I can just work on leveling out the bottom. I set down the shovel to look at my hands. They are sore and blistered in a few areas. My arms ache.

I need to know what time it is and give my hands a break; I don't want to get back to the cabin too late in the day. A quarter-turn of the keys in the ignition of the car shows that it's still only one o'clock. Good; I have plenty of time.

I finish the grave rather quickly now and work through the pain each fling of the shovel delivers. I stand up against the wall to check. It comes right up to my chest. I hoist myself out and lay the ranger's body next to the grave. After lowering myself back in, I pull the ranger off of the ground and lay him gently on the bottom.

Refilling the grave takes half the time of actually digging it. As I finish the mound, I consider making some parting remarks. There are only a few shovel-fulls left.

"Thank you, sir," I begin, weakly. I empty the shovel onto the mound two more times. "You gave us some more time to get on our feet." The last bits of dirt fall from the shovel's edge. "Hopefully we'll be ready by the time it runs out," I say, more to myself than to him.

I'm glad I came back. Something about fulfilling this man's final wishes gives me a sense of belonging here. There are no adults left to do adult's work. I may be about as old as it gets, now. Although that thought is intimidating, I feel a kernel of confidence sprout in my mind that says if anyone can handle this situation now, it's me.

I exhale as if the job is finished, but before I can look away, my thoughts return to my father. Paralyzed, I realize that I'll never have the opportunity to recover his respect, if that was even possible.

"I swear, father." I whisper while staring at the cross on the grave. " I swear that I won't." I mean it. Whatever it takes.

A few moments go by before I relax my grip on the shovel and use my dirty hands to wipe away the tears building in the corner of my eye.

I finished burying my father.

I turn my head toward the tool wall, and after a momentary pause, I collect its contents and pile them in the folded down back seat of the white SUV, including the bow and quiver full of white-finned red arrows. A wooden stop sign about 20 yards into the campground catches my eye. My hand grabs the bow.

I hope you were right about these woods ranger. remembering his note, and the reference to game. I hope the archery club at school taught me enough to do something about it. Despite the pain in my arms and the quarter sized blisters on my hands, I pull back on the string and notch an arrow. My split-finger hold grabs the arrow I take a squared stance, just like I was taught. My arm raises the weapon.

The pain from digging is gone for a single moment, and all I feel is the tension in my leading hand and a focused stillness as I release the arrow.

Chapter 16: Jocelyn

I'm not sure how long it takes to dig a grave, so I try not to worry, but Jon's been gone for a while. Why was he so insistent upon going alone? None of us should be doing anything alone anymore. I'm going to make that a rule when he gets back.

I look toward the window for the thousandth time today to see if there is any hint of orange among the clouds. The clear, bright, blue sky reminds me that it's not as late as my nerves are telling me it is.

The rest of my day so far has involved a walk around the cabin site to get familiar with the nearby area and staring at our food supply trying to figure out how to ration it. "Nutrition for survival in the event of a world-wide catastrophe" was not a topic that was covered in junior year health class this year. I wish it had been. It's going to be very hard to feed the four of us in a way that we don't waste away or go crazy from eating the same things over and over again.

I start to take some kind of inventory of what's here from what Jon organized last night. We have a ton of what appears to be some kind of generic canned pasta, as well as various soups, beans, jarred vegetables, and a few generic larger cans labeled "Chicken-in-a-Can." There is absolutely nothing appetizing about that. My organic diet is about to end. The pantry also holds some kind of perishable items that we'll have to take care of first. We still have a few boxes of those mini-muffins that we had this morning. There's a box on the floor that's full of potatoes, of all things, and a pie tin wrapped in foil sitting on top. I grabbed it the night before off the counter of the station. Either the ranger or his wife did some baking before they passed. I hope it is still good. I peel the foil back and am satisfied that it still seems relatively fresh.

I can't help but smile at the last box that I see. Everyone has always said that Twinkies would be their food of choice in the event of a world-wide catastrophe. I guess we will find out exactly how long they last; two ten-count boxes of Twinkies lay on the top shelf of the pantry. Since Hostess even stopped making them, they could be some of the last real Twinkies in the whole country.

How in the world did we fit all of this in the car last night? I don't remember taking that many trips. Then I realize yesterday was pretty much a blur already.

Eventually, this food will run out. Will we be able to get back to the grocery stores? No. They'll be empty or too dangerous. How long will we have to sustain ourselves here? How can we possibly be expected to do all of this?

"We just have to," I say out loud.

This conclusion feels liberating. The near panic that I had briefly felt was quickly fading away, like a heavy and cold blanket falling from my shoulders. Now, my questions have answers, or at least plans to find them.

I don't know how to farm. How will we grow our food? Trial and error. In the spring we will have to try our best. We have a well-pump, plenty of dirt, and plenty of sun. I start to walk away from the pantry to sit down. And when should we start hunting? It's a long shot, but maybe the stores still have some seeds in them. Maybe people overlooked them in a panic and went for the more conventional products.

Maybe it will not come to that. In the back of my mind I hope things will come together in the country. Jon keeps pushing that this will be our lives for a very long time. Maybe order will be restored with the help of other countries.

I look at the girls. They seem calm right now. I think they're grateful to just have a place to call home again, if even for a little while. If Jon is right, eventually we will need to be living entirely on what we harvest and what we kill. When that time comes, we can't afford to still be learning.

We have bullets. Lots of them. The ranger's rifle and shotgun had several boxes of ammunition next to them. Although it's a substantial supply, it's not infinite. Maybe there's a population of fish in the river that we can use.

Then it occurs to me, I have no idea what the hell I am rambling about. Please God don't let this last long out here.

"Jocelyn? I'm hungry," says Sara, with a half-pout, half-beg on her face.

I put on a warm smile for her. "Don't worry. We can take care of that right now and I have a surprise for you tonight when Jon gets back." That pie isn't going to last long. We might as well celebrate our new home and put some kind of positive spin on this.

"Can... can I have some more muffins?"

"Don't you want something else?" my mind goes to the few bags of chips we brought from our house. Don't all kids want junk food? She shakes her head. "Well, of course you can. Did you like those this morning?" We had some simple soup for lunch, but it obviously wasn't holding them over.

"Yeah," she replies with a timid smile emerging on her face.

"Well good." I give her some and she enjoys them. She offers Sara and me each one as well from the bag. "Ok girls, come here for a second. I want to show you everything that we have. We're going to have to be careful with how quickly we go through these things?" I usher them over to the pantry and show them the shelves. "This will only last the four of us a couple of months at best-so we cannot be wasteful. And if help hasn't arrived by then we're going to have to start relying on other things."

"Like what?" asks Caitlyn.

"Well, Jonathan and I going to try to farm and garden in the spring... and soon we may need to hunt." I'm not sure what kind of reaction that will get, but we're going to have to approach the subject eventually even if I don't know where to start. I also don't know what else to talk about with the girls at the moment...

Sara's eyebrows furl at the word hunt, but Caitlyn has an unexpected reaction; her face shows enthusiasm.

"Can I come?" she asks, clearing her throat afterward.

The words "absolutely not" come to mind. It's not everyday I see such a small girl excited about the concept of killing and eating animals while her excitement should focus around dolls and an opportunity to go to a petting zoo. "Maybe, Caitlyn. Jon and I need to figure it out first."

It's amazing how much an already small child can deflate as she sulks at my response. I guess "maybe" didn't sound too promising in her eyes. Deciding not to give it another thought, I turn back to the pantry and re-stack the boxes of the muffins.

The girls and I take a walk, mostly to get a solid idea of what's immediately around the cabin, but also because I want to get out and breathe. I have felt like I've been holding my breath for days.

The river that I vaguely remember from our family camping trips flows a few dozen yards away from the cabin. The sun sinks over the treetops, and I can't help but think of a short prayer as the sun reflects off the water. My mother and I used to say these, but that habit left with her so many years ago. She was much more religious than my father. Her prayers enter my mind, but I don't know if I believe anymore. Especially after the past few weeks.

I talk with the girls and learn a lot about them. They tell me about themselves, but most of all they tell me about their parents. They were part of a really close family. Sara, as we already learned, is a little more openly confident in herself. She is about an inch taller than Caitlyn and makes sure I know that by reminding us several times as we walked along the creek. It might be their one discernable physical feature. On the emotional side, it seems that Caitlyn still doesn't have as much self-identity yet. I recollect my early middle school years with them, too. I was sure of myself from the age of eight, but Jon was always latching on to new people and trying to be like them. He was never sure of himself until three years ago, and I'm afraid that happened for all the wrong reasons.

We come across a downed log across a shallow part and I balance across it. Sara refuses to try but Caitlyn quickly runs across to me. Then she goes back and tries to drag her sister. Sara resists until Caitlyn gives up. We all laugh and start to make our way back to the cabin. Caitlyn may be more timid, but is much more willing to take chances.

A low rumble comes from the direction of the cabin. We are barely within eye-shot, and it looks like some headlights are shining through the early evening air amongst the shadows of the trees. I need to get back quickly. My heart starts to race at the thought of this car with anyone but Jon. The girls lag behind me as I quickly walk toward our new home.

I breathe a sigh of relief as Jon kills the engine and steps out of the driver's seat. There's a new look in his eye, or a new air about him, or something. Maybe it's the way he's standing. Confidence.

"Hey," he starts, "I picked up some more things from the trailer. We didn't search the outside walls; he had all this equipment. And check this out." He finishes the sentence while throwing open the trunk of the SUV. He reaches in and pulls out a bow.

I know that Jon hates guns, and I always felt like it was strange how involved he was with the archery club when, in my opinion, a gun and bow are so similar. However, I can see how a bow doesn't exactly compare with a gun to Jon...

"The quiver is full, too. This ranger didn't go cheap on them either. The red shafts are carbon. These things will last."

I'm not sure what's so special about carbon, but I let him have his moment. Jon is a good shot, but he isn't exactly Robin Hood. Yet, we have to hunt, and he may be our best chance.

Yea, I better start practicing with the gun.

"That's...really lucky!" I reply, unable to hide my hesitation. "But Jon, do you think..."

"I'll start tomorrow," he interrupts. "It'll take some time."

"We do have the guns."

"You have the guns," he says with a weak smile and raised brow. "The great safari hunter Jo-Jo."

I have hated that name since the second my last boyfriend thought of it. Jon heard it once and likes to use it to get under my skin.

That boyfriend lasted three days after that.

Anyway, hunting was not really what I wanted to hear. I'm completely clueless when it comes to bows, and I'm not much better when it comes to guns. "You said equipment. What else did you find?"

"Take a look."

I walk around the car, and for what feels like the first time in forever, I exhale a little bit deeply and smile. Now there is a little bit of luck as he shows me the variety of gardening tools.

"All we need are some seeds and a place to put them," he continues. "Come spring, we are going to rock this land." His trip has encouraged him. It feels good knowing that both of us are focused.

"We need to start immediately planning for when winter ends," I say after nodding for a moment. "I went over the pantry. It could barely get us through the winter, but then we will be on our own."

"I know. I measured it out a little bit last night and I don't even thing it will last that long. Until we learn what it means to hunt and farm, we are going to need more. We should head..." his last words trail off. I know what he's going to say, so I let myself sigh. Tension replaces our optimism. "We need to go to that grocery store."

"When do you want to go?" I ask. It was dangerous, but he was right. The amount of food we have would be cutting it too close this winter.

"Tomorrow. We leave before the sun rises. I want to get there as early as possible without it being dark and before more people get a chance to rummage through it."

"I'm not letting you go alone."

"We all will go."

"What about the girls?" I ask while glancing toward the window. They are both inside fiddling with something.

Jon fixes his posture and exhales. "You stay with them in the car. We'll have to park far enough away from the store so that nobody sees it. I'll take our bags, go in, and grab as much as I can. You can honk if you see something or get me out of there quickly if things turn bad."

He's right; I should stay with the girls, but I am so uncomfortable with the thought of him going in there alone. "No. We should come, too."

He shakes his head. "You know that's not the best move. Someone has to stay with the car. That's that."

I purse my lips. There's nothing to argue here. We make our way into the cabin and the twins are relieved to chat with him again. They have been drawing on some paper from one of our bags.

"So when's dinner?" Sara asks. She looks at me. To be honest, I did not even think about getting anything ready. "What are we having?"

"Well Sara," I begin, "we'll have something ready soon!" I nod to Jon. He shakes his head and puts his hands up. Neither of us can cook.

Great start to our survival.

"Let's have some of this canned pasta." I say as I grab a can off the shelf. "and then: pumpkin pie!"

It doesn't take long to open up two cans of the pasta and heat them over the stove. With the cans open, the pie laid out, and some silverware on the table, everyone digs in. It still feels good to look around and see smiles after so many meals these past weeks with entirely blank and tired faces. The main course is gone in a flash.

"Who's going to cut the pie?" asks Caitlyn, with an excitement flashing across her face.

"I want a big piece!" exclaims Sara, with the same glee sparkling in her eyes.

"Hold on, girls! I'll take care of it," I say. I cut the pie into eight equal slices. I'm debating whether or not we should just eat the whole thing now.

The table is quiet during dessert except for the sound of voracious chewing and a few giggles. Once half the pie is gone, everyone at the table silently makes eye contact with each other before digging into the other half.

Chapter 17: Jonathon

My familiar cell phone morning jingle wrenches me out of unconsciousness. It won't be long until we can't depend on the cell phone alarm. The battery drained as it tried desperately to acquire a signal, so I slipped it into the car charger yesterday. We can't hope for it to work too much longer. For now it will do. Someday, even battery-powered alarms will be useless; there will be no batteries.

I can see that it stirs the girls, and Jo shoots up quickly. I've done that before, but usually after anticipating something intimidating all night. With any luck it won't go wrong and we won't see anybody there this morning.

Rolling out of bed, I call to Sara and Caitlyn. "All you have to do is come to the car, girls," I say, conveying how easy it will be once they're there. "You can fall right back to sleep in the back, okay?" Their eyes don't really open fully, but they stumble out of their bunks and slowly slide what looks like clown-sized jackets over their arms. Jo's clothing will have to keep working for now.

Jo is shaking her head to clear it. She could probably do with a little bit more sleep as well. "I'll drive," I say, grabbing the keys from the table and walking to the door. We pile into the SUV after I lock the cabin door behind us, but I doubt anyone will even be in the area. Caitlyn coughs in the back seat as she and her sister nestle together. I start the engine and slowly guide the vehicle out of the campground so that the bumps don't disturb the girls too much. Before long, we're on the open road, headed toward the civilization that just two days ago we would've given anything to leave completely behind.

The ride is long, and the sun is just beginning to turn the starlit sky into a deep blue in the east. The soft breathing and infrequent stirring of the girls provides a little bit of a distraction, or at least a reminder of what's at stake here. If I can fill these backpacks with food, we'll last this winter. We just need enough time to get some sort of system in place.

Thoughts of hunting and gardening stir my mind until I notice the familiar signs for the nearby town. I know that super center is up on the hill not far from here, so I pull the car off the road and swing it into the brush.

Jo stirs. "Are we here?"

"Yes. Here are the keys. Turn your phone on and give me an hour. If I'm not back by then, head back to the cabin."

"Jon, we aren't..."

"Yes you will," I whisper. "Besides," I start, smiling, "If I get tied up I will just run the mega-marathon." I slap the side of my thigh twice. "Like a horse."

She looks back at me, obviously not amused. "Be careful," she insists. I nod.

I drop the keys on the driver's seat, pull the three backpacks out of the passenger seat foot-well, and start off. By putting two backpacks inside of the third, I'm able to strap it on and jog off in the direction of the grocery store. The sun is over the horizon now, but it hasn't been long. We've timed it well.

The hike to the parking lot is short. In ten minutes, I'm approaching the asphalt. The store is up on a hill, so I crouch as I reach the crest. Needlessly, I slyly raise my head above the crest. No cars in the lot. No people walking out the doors. It looks like the doors themselves are broken. The large parking lot looks empty compared to a few days ago. All that's left is some twirling trash.

I increase my jog to a run to get across the parking lot. It's eerie; I've never seen a twenty four hour store so completely dead.

Just like the bodies that are keeping the front doors open.

My run comes to an abrupt halt as I notice them at the entrance; a few are bloody and twisted. I draw a deep breath and force it out through tight lips. Some of the bodies are not very old. The holes in the door windows look like they were from bullets. Is this going on all over the country?

I'm here for a purpose. Get in, get out, get back to the cabin so we can completely withdraw. I try not to look at their faces as I quietly walk through the entryway. Some of them are five...maybe even ten...years younger than me, but I force myself to look up.

It's pretty clear that this store had been cleared by those looters, but it hasn't been emptied. The cashier lanes even have some protein bars left on their shelves. I don't have much time, but I grab one to quickly eat as I proceed. I find the canned food aisle sign and head there. The lights inside keep flickering on and off. Along the way, I start to become aware of the smell of the place. I toss the remainder of the bar to the ground. There are some corpses scattered about the store, but not nearly as densely as they are at the entryway. I can't help but speculate that these were people that came in, collected bags, and had them taken from them as they tried to leave. I notice some bullet holes and blood along the walls. Those with guns took what they wanted.

I hate guns.

I pass a few shelves full of medicine, and I fill the smallest pouches of my bag with the bottles that I recognize. Aspirin, Ibuprofen, and some general decongestants will help when the temperature drops or allergies kick in. I'm not even sure how to use anything else. The pharmacy is on my left, and I hop through the window. The doctors always prescribe penicillin tablets for infections, so I'll grab some of those. I jump back through the window and proceed to the food. The next few aisles are freezer aisles, and with the electricity on and off, their contents are probably spoiled.

The canned food aisle, predictably, is one of the more empty ones. However, considering that I only have three backpacks, just enough cans remain spread along the floor and under some of the shelves to fill my first bag . Some cans are pretty dented, but they should still be okay. Once I have that one on my back, I take another glance under some other shelves and continue. This should work perfectly; enough things have been left behind amidst the violence. There appears to be just enough to fill these backpacks. On the way out, I'll grab some more candy bars for the girls. This went better than I...

Steps.

Up until now, the only thing demanding the attention of my ears has been the flicker of the lights. But now I hear footsteps coming from the front of the store. I quickly consider the worst-case scenario: a hungry, bigger man sees me with three full backpacks in an otherwise empty canned food aisle. There's nowhere to hide, and I'm not putting these things down. I turn and try to quietly escape to the back of the store, slowly watching where I place each step.

"Hey," I hear from behind me. I'm not going to outrun anybody with all of this extra weight. I stop and turn around.

"What do you have there in those bags?" growls the figure standing at the end of the aisle. He is the worst case scenario. He's tall and probably a year or two older than I am but he has a boyish face with expression that is very unsettling. His body is square with the width of the aisle, but his head is turned partially to the side, making his dark eyes appear even more accusing from under his heavy brow. He is the size of an ox.

"Almost everything in this store is gone. I think there is some more over in that aisle." I reply, pointing away, and hoping to evade the obvious and true answer to his question.

"That's not what I asked," he boomed, beginning to take heavy strides down the aisle. "What's in your bags?"

I need to get this food to the girls – to Jo. I can't give anything up. I have to convince this man that it's all for me and he can't have any.

That'll go over well.

"I asked you a question!" he roared, taking quicker steps, clenching his fists.

"Just a few cans," I admit. "I need them," I add weakly while backing up a few steps at a time.

"Not as badly as I do. Give them to me."

"I can't. You don't understand."

"Give them to me!" he roared again.

"Listen, I need these!" I yell back. "Can we just talk…"

"Give them to me!" His walk turns into a run, and the snarl on his face makes him appear to be more of an animal than a man. I hope I was wrong about being able to outrun him.

I turn and head for the next aisle over, and run as fast as I can toward the front of the store. The weight of the bags in my arms prevents my arms from swinging, so I just lean as far forward as I can and try to stay balanced. This is what it feels like to run for your life.

His face greets me as I approach the front of the aisle, followed by his fist. How stupid am I? Did I really believe he wouldn't just turn around and block the exit? I stagger back and turn to run the other way, but he tackles me, trying to pry the backpacks out of my hands. The time for talk is over.

I let go of the bag in my right hand and deliver a cross to his left eye. I guess he didn't anticipate that I'd fight back, so the strike shocks him for a moment. I roll back up and grab the pack on the ground, and turn around to find my exit. As I turn around, I raise my left arm just in time to deflect another punch with a bag. He yells in anger as his knuckles glance off the cans inside. His other hand swings into the side of my face and my vision blurs for a second. I get ready to block more punches, but he doesn't swing. He lunges for my neck.

With my hands weighed down, there is no way I am going to keep his fingers from wrapping around my throat. My knees bend and I try to keep on my feet. He'll kill me. A wave of panic and rage surges through my body as I open my hands, letting the two bags fall to the ground. He shoves me against the shelves. My hands shoot to his wrists, but are unable to pluck them away. Instead, I raise my hands above my head and bring my thumbs into his eyes. I push as hard as I can. His hands and arms release from the pain, and I can draw a full breath. I grab his shirt at the shoulder and under the other arm and deliver a knee to his groin.

His hands immediately release my neck completely and I back away, grabbing the two bags on the ground. He staggers over to one of the shelf units and supports himself on one of the items. I turn and run down the new aisle I find myself in.

Of course. The cutlery aisle.

I turn and see him ripping the plastic coating off of a paring knife and he charges at me with a new-found energy. He quickly catches up. I let the packs slide to the floor again and try to dodge his attack at the same time. The knife slices through my right sleeve and the skin under it. I see red beginning to darken my coat. I wish I had put the gun in my pocket. I thought I would be safer without it. Wrong. I reach for anything on the shelves that I can and start throwing at him to slow him.

A cheese grater.

A plastic cutting board.

A potato peeler.

Finally, I find myself with a pan in one hand, and I'm reaching for a mop with the other. This would be funny if I wasn't about to die.

As he jumps at me, I shove the mop in his face-the absorbent side. He uses both hands to shove it to his left. I let go of the mop with my left hand, and while spinning clockwise I deliver a blow with the edge of the pan to the left side of his head. I've never put so much effort into a swing in my life.

It lands just behind his eye with a sickening crack. The edge breaks through the skin, and his eyes roll back into his head as his body crumbles to the ground. My legs are locked for a moment, and my breathing is labored as my focus remains on the deep wound that I've left in the side of his skull.

I bend down and reach for his neck with my left hand. With two fingers across his throat, I wait, feeling for any kind of signal that his heart is still beating.

Nothing. I look at the pan. The edge is crimson, and noticeably dented from the force of the blow. Dropping it to the floor, I collect the bags while breathing harder and harder. A pool of blood forms around his head. I try to feel guilty, but it was just like Darry on the city street. He deserved this, maybe that's why I don't feel sick this time. Not shooting Darry made me sick.

Killing wasn't that hard...

The girls. I need to get back. Do I have everything I need? I look back at the aisle and realize that some of these items could be invaluable. I put one bag over each shoulder and one in my left hand so that my right is free for a big pot with some knives and other items. I step over the recent corpse to grab a metal spatula.

There are movies, mints, books, and some other stands in front of the cash registers. Useless. I need to make sure we have everything we need. One of the stands in particular catches my eye.

Seeds. The stand is full of seeds with a big clearance sign on top of it. Nobody has taken these yet. What's more, one register over, there's a stand of books with titles like "Paint Your Thumb Green" and "Gardening for Dummies." I shove as many seeds as I can in the gaps in the bags, which turns out to be substantial, and I put a few books under my arm. The last thing I need is another encounter. I wobble out of the store with all of my goodies in every nook possible on my body.

The rest of the trip back to the car goes without a hitch. When I am almost to the SUV, I stumble and fall down the small hill, dropping the books and one of the backpacks. I look up from the ground and see Jo running toward me.

When she asks how it went I think I will leave out the boy I killed.

Chapter 18: Caitlyn

This is the second time that Jon's gone away, and it's scarier than the first. He could get hurt this time. I keep falling asleep in the car, and I feel so cold. Jocelyn and Sara are talking about something, but I have no interest. Something about Jon. Both of them seem okay, so I bundle Jo's coat a little tighter. I feel an itch in my throat and cough.

"Are you okay?" Jocelyn asks from the driver's seat.

"I wanna go soon. Do you see Jon?"

"He'll be back soon," she replies, rolling back into her seat to get a better look where Jon ran off. She quickly shoots upright, though, and I follow her eyes to see Jon falling down the hill, with much more than the three backpacks in tow. Jo runs out to meet him. Sara giggles for a second. He looks so foolish carrying all that stuff and then rolling down the hill. Sara and I both climb out of the car to help.

"Jon!" she yells, reaching his side. Jon seems briefly dizzy, and Jo picks up two of the backpacks as the two hurry to the car. I begin to pick up a few cans that rolled to the bottom. With all our efforts we have the car loaded up. As Jon shuts the door, a smudge of red covers the trunk handle.

"Jon, you're hurt." Sara whimpers. "Your arm." Jon lifts it to his eyes.

"Oh, this? I scraped it along one of the aisles trying to grab more stuff. I will cover it when we get back. It was so dark inside. The place was empty-completely different from 48 hours ago." Sara looks relieved but something doesn't feel right about his story.

We scramble into the vehicle and head back to the cabin. I don't want to, but I can't keep myself from coughing. I try to be quiet the whole way home, but eventually Sara tugs at my shirt.

"Are you okay?" she asks. I try to smile and nod. Jon isn't fooled, and he looks back at me from the passenger's seat.

"What's wrong, Cait? Do you need some water?"

"No."

"Are you sure? How do you feel?"

My lips drop into a frown. "Bad."

"We're not far from home. We'll get you back under the covers and you'll feel much better, ok? You probably just need some good rest and a real meal. Jo will take care of you, right Jo?"

Jo looks away from the road for a second and rolls her eyes. Their interactions remind me of mom and dad sometimes. They have trouble being serious for too long. Sara likes that. I don't.

I keep my frown. "Ok."

The ride drags on, and each pothole makes my head hurt more and more. It's not even noon yet, and all I want is to go back to sleep. Maybe tomorrow I'll wake up and feel better.

After glancing at me a few times, Jo just keeps looking over at her brother and inhaling like she wants to start saying something, but she never does. I think it is about me.

Eventually, I drift back to sleep with my head in Sara's lap.

The car comes to an abrupt stop, and I wake up just as quickly. We're home, and Jon wasn't very soft on the brakes. My throat hurts really badly, and I have to cringe to swallow. I let out another whimper, stretching and trying to make the soreness in my arms and legs go away.

We head into the cabin and Jocelyn tucks me into bed. Jon grabs the first aid kit and sets it on the table. He takes off his coat so that he can tend to his cut. Jocelyn and Sara begin to store some of the stuff Jon found away but after awhile she asks Sara to go outside and fill one of the buckets with water at the pump. I try to close my eyes and fall asleep.

When I hear the door slam, there is a moment of silence. I keep my eyes closed but I hear both of them whisper to one another.

"Jon, what really happened to your arm? Your face looks puffy, too.'

"I'm telling the truth"

"Don't lie to me."

"I'm not!" Their voices begin to get louder.

"Jon you don't just fall and get a cut on your arm and the beginning of a black eye. Tell me the truth. Now."

"I fell while the lights were flickering. Leave it the hell alone."

"How can we expect to make it if you're not even honest with me?"

"I am honest with you. You're the only thing I care about in this screwed up world."

"Then why are you lying?" They are nearly yelling at one another.

"This is the truth. Now leave...it...alone."

"You're unbelievable." She swears at him.

Listening to Jo and Jon argue is kind of scary. I can feel my heart beating. The more I focus on it, though, the quicker it slows down. That just lets my mind go back to my chills and headache. It takes some time, but I'm finally able to shut my eyes and drift into an uncomfortable sleep.

* * *

Each day I feel worse and worse. Almost a week has gone by since I started to feel awful. My head feels like it is on fire but I feel cold at the same time.

Initially, they worried that maybe I had gotten the plague somehow. Jo checked every inch of me for the rash, but she said I was clear. The possibility of having the plague made me really upset, so it was relieving to know that it was something else. Jon and Jocelyn have looked over a few book s they found in the ranger's cabin, but so far they haven't been able to figure out what is wrong with me. We have all the medicine, but they are each afraid to give me anything. So my job is to stay in bed and eat when I can and hope that the ibuprofen is enough.

I look outside and see the three of them messing with the ground. Jon has an idea to try and get a few things grown before it gets too cold. They do look funny out there fooling around in the dirt.

Chapter 19: Jonathon

All I can do right now is keep her comfortable, hydrated, and fed. The penicillin that we took from the store is starting to seem more and more like an option, though. I know there is a difference between prescription and over the counter drugs, and I don't know the consequences of using a prescription drug incorrectly. There has to be a reason that only doctors can allow you to get them. I hope she will get better naturally.

Everything else is settling into a rhythm. Jo, Sara, and I are all reading up on gardening, and we've planted some of the radish seeds that can be harvested in as few as four weeks – according to one of those books anyway. It didn't seem like a bad idea to take our first slug at gardening in the last month before winter. We can't find any other plants that grow so quickly inside of that time frame.

I hope I like radishes. I see a lot of them in my future.

Jo and Sara are looking out the window, talking about what the trees look like when they just start to change color.

"I'll bet the first one to be completely bare will be that one," says Sara, pointing to a big maple tree about eighty feet away from the house.

"Alright," replies Jo. "I'll take that one," she said, pointing to another tree a little further away as Sara presses her face against the glass.

"Don't forget which one you picked," Sara exclaimed. She turns to me with a smile and I smile back, she quickly turns to look back out the window. It sounds like a silly wager to me. They stared out the window a lot and hoped to see animals. Maybe it was replacing TV.

Caitlyn stirs and Sara hops away from the window sill to tend to her sister. The sun is approaching the western hilltops, so we probably only have a few hours of daylight left. Now's a good a time as any to start dinner.

Jo must have read my mind. "What do you feel like cooking today?" she asks, walking over to the table.

"What I feel like cooking? You mean what do you feel like cooking?" I argue.

My sister lazily glares at me and I look to the closed pantry and think of what we have. Those pots and tools that we'd gotten at the grocery store are fantastic. Along with the few pieces of kitchenware from the ranger's station, we have all that we'll need to last the winter.

"Let's do pasta tonight." I've become pretty good at draining the water from the pot with just the lid, and I'm feeling pretty hungry.

"Again?" Sara complains. "We have had that like four times already" She says at the foot of Caitlyn's bed. Caitlyn seems to be asleep again at the moment.

"Well do you have any ideas?"

"As a matter of fact...I do." She hops down off the bed and grabs the pantry door. She talks to herself briefly. "Now if I remember from mom..." she grabs a few random cans and boxes and sets them down on the table. She sits for a second and stares at them. I watch in amusement – she is determined.

"Where are the spices and everything?" she asks. I point to the cabinet. I watch as she struggles on her toes to reach for the top shelf. I come up behind her and bring them down.

"I could have reached them, Jonathon."

"Oh I know, just consider me your sous chef."

"What's that?" she asks, opening the ranger's array of seasonings and spices.

"Your assistant." She smiles and begins to lay down her plan of how we are going to add a little of this with a little of that and come out with some sort of stew. I help her open some cans and gather some fresh water. She takes a third of a box, mixes it in, and begins to stir.

She has no idea what she is doing.

"Okay, now sous-chef Jon. Let this cook for 15 minutes. Now, I also want to prepare those instant mashed potatoes." She turns to her sister. "This should all be easy for her to eat."

She rips open the pouch and I begin to heat some more water over the stove. While she is distracted with the potatoes I grab a spoon from the drawer and taste the stew. I may need to add a little, a lot, of seasoning when she is not looking. However, when I bring it to my mouth, it tastes alright. Maybe she does have an idea.

"Pretty good!" I say with a grin and a thumbs-up.

"Of course," she turns with a smile.

The two of us finish preparing the meal while Jo sets the table and checks on Caitlyn. We serve the meal onto the dishes on the table and we take turns helping Caitlyn eat. When she feels up to it, we prop her up in her bed and sit with her as she slurps away at the stew. She manages to eat half of it. The plates at the table get completely cleaned.

"Good work, Sara" replies Jo rising to her feet. She sets her plates down and walks to the corner. "I'm sure you two won't mind doing cleanup, too. I'm headed out."

"Out? Who's the guy?" I ask. Sara and I begin to collect the plates and put them in a wash bucket already heating on the stove.

She snickers as she grabs the rifle from the corner. "Hopefully, 'he' is an 'it', and 'it' is going to die."

"Isn't it a little dark to try to be a great hunter Jo-Jo?"

"It's as good a time as any."

Our uncle always used to talk about hunting at the very crack of dawn. There must have been a reason for that. "Can't we wait until tomorrow? I will come."

"Just relax, we've an hour left."

"Why are you pushing this now?" I ask moving closer.

"Because," she begins, lowering her voice, "I'm tired of you doing pretty much everything around here."

"You know I don't see it like that," I argue. The tension rises.

"Well I do."

"We haven't even fired one of those guns yet. What if someone hears it? Think."

"I am thinking. It will be fine. Stay with them."

"Jocelyn, you are acting like a child." It slips before I can hold it in.

"No. I've never been a child because I have always had to put up with you." She sighs. We are both angry. This is how most conversations went before the plague came along. She speaks loud so the twins can now hear. "Jon, I'm going, I'll see you soon."

"Girls, I'm going for a walk. I'll see you in an hour." she says, slinging the gun over her shoulder and heading to the door. I don't think she would ever admit it, but I think she was jealous of Sara and me preparing dinner.

It was my fault, too. I'm still just trying to make up these past few years. How can I make up for taking mom away from her?

"Bye!" the twins say in unison, only one is much weaker than the other.

"Don't go too far!" I call out after Jo.

"Yes, sir!" replies Jo, saluting me with disdain.

After a little bit of work, I get a fire growing in the stove and grab the big basin from the stove top with the dinner's dishes inside. Sara and I dry the dishes together and she helps me stack them neatly on the table.

"Do you need me to do anything else?" she asks willingly. She wants to help me more.

"No, go play." I add.

"With what?" she inquires while shrugging her shoulders and putting her hands in the air. She smiles.

"Be creative."

"Oh, alright." She grins and jumps to the other bunk and fiddles with something.

I grab the basin to rinse it outside. The pump is just around the side of the cabin, and with only a few pumps, it loyally spouts cool well water. God help us if this thing breaks.

I muse for a little bit too long over the mechanics of a spout, and some water spills out of the tipped pot, splashing freezing water onto my ankles. A few curses escape my mouth as I shake the water from the bucket. I turn back toward the cabin. It is getting darker much more quickly than I expected.

More quickly than I'm sure Jo had expected, too.

As I round the house with the basin in hand, something catches my eye and I step back up behind the corner. A dark figure moved among some trees. Was it an animal? My eyes squint. The person moves again. I slowly set down the bucket.

"No… not right now," I whisper to myself. After peeking around again, I see that he's walking with his head down. He may not have seen me.

The answer is all too obvious as the wisps of smoke blowing from the chimney grab my attention- he's here for our food and supplies. The images of the raging man at the grocery store come back to my mind. I won't give him the opportunity to harm the girls. There will be no talking this time. I need to act first.

Fifty feet. The man is pretty clear, now. He looks to be a bit shorter than six feet, but in reasonable shape. There's a hiking backpack strapped to him which could slow him down significantly. He walks slowly and slightly crouched, with his gaze almost directly at his feet. Maybe he doesn't want to be seen-maybe he doesn't want to scare anyone? No. he's trying to hide. He wants to sneak up on us.

That's it. Once he's past that corner, I'll close the gap and take him out.

Switching to the other back corner of the house, I watch as he nears the opposite front corner, still walking toward the door. He lifts his head up, apparently making sure he's still headed in the right direction. I will have a few moments where his back will be toward me as he goes to the door.

He seems tired. It makes no difference. He won't know what hit him. Three... two... one...

He passes the corner, and I'm at a dead sprint. Even if he hears me at this point, it's going to take a second to register, and I'll be on top of him. He's only a quarter of the way through turning around, and I've left the ground, my shoulder lined up with his gut and my hands extend for his wrists.

"Oof!" I hear as my shoulder drives the breath out of his body. He goes down easily, as the backpack is already weighing him down. I've gotten my right hand around his left wrist. With my left, I deliver a jab across his face to stun him. I release with my right hand and tighten it into a fist, bringing it crashing down onto him. The backpack is keeping his hips off the ground, making it difficult for him to kick me, and the right strap is preventing him from delivering anything but a weak cross with his right arm. I shrug off one of these and continue to pummel him.

His right hand stops swinging, and instead it comes across his face in an effort to deflect some of my blows. I grab that wrist with my left hand, and press it to the ground above his head while I raise my right shoulder for a final blow.

His head recoils, and he fiercely grimaces. All of a sudden, I feel his right arm pushing with much greater strength against my left hand. His groan becomes a scream of aggression as his arm comes slowly off the ground, bringing my hand with it.

A rock lies next to his head, and just as he inhales for another burst of effort, I grab the rock and raise it high in the air. I'll finish this just like the last time.

My hand with the rock comes wheeling forward, aiming for that same point in front of the ear.

Chapter 20: Carter

Finally making it to the campground is a relief.

It brings back memories of my family. I miss them. I came here with my father and mother for as long as I can remember. He always inspired me, and my mother always supported me. Other than a brief moment when I was eight and I fired a potato gun through our den window, I had a loving childhood. They both pushed me to be exceptional. Dad worked his way through medical school thus he accepted nothing less than my best every time. He signed me up for every rec sport and scouting program my hometown had to offer.

However, his strictness and discipline paid off when middle school, apparently one of the most difficult times for a child, moved me on to ninth grade a year early. High school and my pre-med program were similarly abbreviated, but I wouldn't have minded those lasting a little bit longer. It's tough making friends when you're the youngest child in school and one of the few black kids.

Once I was older, responsibility loomed over me as I scraped through the first year of med school and worked as a city EMT. Free hours were few and far between, but mom and dad were proud of their hardworking boy. I still called their house home and they didn't mind.

It was midsummer and some of my friends from home were getting together for a little trip. I decided to take a brief vacation from work to celebrate the end of my summer classes with them by trekking through the south. Backpacking through Georgia wasn't my idea, but it seemed like it could be fun.

"It's good you are taking a bit of a vacation. You really are running yourself thin." said my mother, with a pleasant smile on her face. Her hair was beginning to look gray against her ebony skin, but her energy always engulfed those around her.

"Yeah, aren't you supposed to be done already with classes by now? It took me one summer to get to my residency," jested my father, behind a worn newspaper.

"Not everyone can bribe the professors," I answered.

He chuckled again. "Well played. It did get expensive." He gazed seriously to the top of the room. If I didn't know better, it would look like he actually had cheated his way through school. It was my turn to laugh. Being a doctor was tradition in my family. His father, my grandfather, was the first and had been the target of racism when he went through med school. Matters got worse when he married my grandma, who was white. However, they claim this all made them stronger and helped to make my father the man he is today.

Thus making me the man I am today.

"So before you get too packed," my mother joined in, "we have a small present for you in the closet."

"Oh?"

"Look in your closet." Dad said putting down the paper.

I stood up and opened my closet door to find an enormous, new hiking pack. I had one from my youth, but this one was much better.

"It's a fifty-eight liter model. You can fit more junk and it lacks the array of holes the old one has." said my dad.

I felt a smile creep across my face. "This is fantastic. Thank you, both, so much."

"And now you can carry a little bit of us with you wherever you go." My mom always had a way of making things uncomfortably cheesy. After that, I hurried and finished packing, and said my goodbyes.

I wish I had given them a longer goodbye.

Seven days later, after finishing my trip and saying goodbye to my friends, I was driving back to the house, looking forward to a long, long shower. Between the blasting radio and my tone deaf singing, I barely heard the fire truck screaming up behind me. I thought nothing of it until I came around the corner and saw it stop in front of my parent's house.

That image etched itself in my mind like how a laser etches metal. I jumped out of the car, and entered a furious sprint for our house.

It was in flames.

"What's going on?" I screamed to one of the firemen over the sound of the flames and the water from the fire truck. "Are my parents out?"

"A neighbor called it in. Said she believed that the they were home, but hadn't seen them. Kid…"

I didn't care what he had to say after that- I was running for the front door. Where would they be? It was late. Did they fall asleep already? They must have. That means they're stuck on the second floor...

I didn't get to finish that thought. Halfway to the front of the house, the entry way collapsed, and with it came some of the second floor. My shock made me pause, giving the firemen enough time to catch up and haul me back to the trucks.

"Son," began one of the firemen, panting, "We've never seen a house go up so fast. If anyone's in there... I'm sorry."

Their bodies were never even found.

So after the services, I buried myself in work. Quickly I found an apartment next to the emergency response station and lived off of mostly what was in my pack from my trip. Nearly everything else I owned was stuck in the house. I took double shift after double shift, and even pulled triples with coffee and cigarettes. For nearly two months I lived like this.

Then the plague came.

At first it just meant long hours, something I was used to, but then it evolved into something ugly. Ugly doesn't even cut it: something horrific. People would fight over who would get into our ambulance. Strong-arming people out of the way after we loaded a patient into the back of the bus became the usual. Soon, that changed to leaving nearly anyone who had the plague. The hospital was full and we were just to stabilize people and only transport the critical cases. Then things became even worse. Some parts of the city were losing power and water. The instinctual drive for survival was becoming evident across many of the children that I passed. Children rummaged through the trash and I even stumbled upon some of them looting. Some were like animals running along side our ambulance.

A few weeks into the plague, the paramedic and I were at a gas station refilling the ambulance. Gas had fallen into short supply and only emergency vehicles could get fuel at certain stations. We just have to tell them how much to put on at the pump.

"I'll be right back," said my partner, headed in to pre-pay.

"Sure," I said in reply, lighting up a cigarette.

I took a long drag before smothering the cigarette in the ash tray. It'd been a long night already and we had hours yet to go. I kept trying to quit, but the fire and the plague suspended that indefinitely. Martin, my partner for this day, came back and put in the nozzle. I didn't know him too well. People tended to call him Marty.

"I'm going back in. You want anything?" he asked.

"I'm cool man." I respond trying to lean back and stretch my lower back. Calls were coming through the radio. I turned it down for a second. By my count I had been working for thirty hours straight.

I was watching the dial climb on the fuel gauges when a few loud pops seized my attention. They came from inside the shop. In the few seconds that it took for my mind to register what was happening, two more bangs emanated from the store. I slouched deep in my seat as a weak attempt to hide. I couldn't hear anything from inside, so I raised my torso just high enough to peek out the window. The shop was a dozen yards away at most. Through a potato chip stand, I could see the cashier collapsed over the counter, Martin sprawled out on the floor, and a boy, no older than 15, running out the back with a large duffel bag. I rushed in and turned my partner onto his back, but it was too late. He was already gone. The cashier also had two bullets straight through his chest.

The opened register caught my attention. All the money was still inside. I looked around and noticed all of the empty beef jerky boxes beside the register. The nearby refrigerator's bottled water supply seemed under-stocked.

People were surviving no matter what the cost.

I would see the aftermath of three more robberies before I gave up working. Most of the city's emergency medical services had stopped working anyway. Everyone was either dead or dying. By all rights, I should be dead, too.

I was twenty-two, and the magic number seemed to be nineteen.

When I walked through the streets for the last time I passed crowds of kids looking for help. I felt selfish as I pushed through the crying children and over the occasional body on the pavement to get back to my new apartment. As I turned into the front entrance I saw a pack of teenagers rip some others out of a car, knock them around, and then steal the vehicle. I needed to get out of the city.

As I walked up the steps, I passed a deceased police officer. He was sitting against the wall. His uniform seemed to be stuck to his body with blood and sweat. That damn rash covered his entire face and his eyes were locked wide open. My fingers found the top of his eyelids and pulled them down. It looks like he was trying to do his job until the very end. He was a better man than me.

My eyes trailed down to his waist, to his gun. After debating for a moment, I undid the buckle and took the entire belt. I figured the radio, the cuffs, and the gun would all come in handy. After checking the gun, I dropped them into my bag and continued to my room. My plan was to pack everything in my hiking backpack and get out of the city, go to the campground, and wait this out until international aid rolls in.

I journeyed for what felt like days – over the bridge, through the tunnel, through neighborhood after neighborhood. Sometimes I slept in abandoned houses, and other times I lied under the stars. I did my best to avoid people at any cost. It took two visits to grocery stores along the way to realize that people had changed. I had to wait just within visible distance of the grocery stores to wait out the chaos of daylight and early night. Whatever humanity had once existed was gone. In its place were animals: these new children that only cared about survival. Any relevance to civility died when every adult in America died.

When I finally made it to the campground, I went to the park's station. Will had always been friendly with my father when we would come up here. I was sure he was dead, but maybe his trailer would be a start. To my dismay it was empty.

Surprisingly, it looked like he had been buried out back. The gate was locked, too.

Someone had shared in my idea.

I decided to spend the night here last night. I wake up feeling very fatigued. My limited diet from the journey has taken its toll on me. I shake my head, clear my thoughts, and consider my course of action for the day.

After spending a night in the ranger's cabin, I journey through the campground. The whole property is hundreds of acres and someone could be living on any piece of it. This is my job today: to find them.

Just as the sun is about to set, I pass over a hill and see smoke rising from one of the cabins against the darkening blue sky. I feel relief as I make my way closer to scope it out. Peering through the window with my binoculars, I see two little girls and a couple of older ones. The older girl eventually ends up walking out with a rifle on her back. That catches me off guard, so for a moment, I continue hiding in the trees. It's already darkening and I couldn't really make out her face. It seems she is going to hunt. An odd time for that.

After she is far enough away, I turn back to the cabin. The older boy has disappeared but I imagine he is somewhere inside. I make up my mind to just casually approach the cabin. They seem nice enough. Maybe they could help me out for a night or two. My stomach lets out a small growl. I walk slowly to the front door, my back slightly hunched from my pack.

Behind me I hear a rustling of grass. Someone was running and before I can completely turn around, a shoulder drives into my stomach and throws me to the ground. It is the boy from inside the cabin.

He wrestles my hands as I try to push him away.

Please stop. I'm not going to hurt you. I am too busy blocking his blows to get the words out. He lands a few hits to my face, but I have been hit much harder than this before.

"Please… stop…" I finally utter through gritted teeth between trying to deflect his fists. He ignores me and I see his right hand reaching for something. He raises up a rock that has been lying next to me. It reaches an apex high above his shoulder and he rips it down toward my head.

I instinctively wrench my head to the left. The rock grazes the right side of my brow.

Enough.

His miss with the rock leaves him unbalanced and I lift both of my feet and kick him straight off me. As he falls back my hands go to my chest, undoing the pack's harness and freeing it from my torso. I leap to my feet and take a fighting stance.

"Listen buddy, I don't wanna hurt you!" I yell. He lunges at me with a fist, but it's sloppy. He probably hasn't been in too many fights in his life. I lean to the right, and he stumbles as he misses. I'm not going to draw this out; my left foot kicks out in front of his ankles and he trips to the ground. I pin him immediately. I place my knee over his throat and restrain his hands. His legs kick fruitlessly. Now maybe we can talk.

"Get off him now!" a voice screams. I look up to see a rifle a few feet from my head. Well maybe we can't talk.

"Woah, I was just trying to get him to calm down," I plea while standing up holding up both hands. My gun is in my bag and useless to me at this moment. The boy gets to his feet and is coughing. The young girls I saw earlier in the window open the front door and light showers the three of us. I can see everyone clearly now.

"Who the hell are you?" the boy asks. He may be around eighteen. His shaggy brown hair falls partly over his brown eyes that manage to convey a burning fire. He has a slim frame, but as my probably bruised face just learned, he can manage a punch or two. I turn to the girl. She's around the same age. Her hair is somewhere between blonde and red and... she's beautiful. Despite the fact that she is probably about to shoot me, she is a sight I have not seen in a long, long time. I raise my hands higher and begin my plea:

"The name's Carter. I'm from the city. I used to come here when I was a kid and I thought this would be a safe place to hold out until this flies by." They exchanges looks, and I sense that they don't believe me. "I swear. I mean you no harm. I saw the lights and thought maybe you could help me out for a few days."

The girl begins to lower her gun. The boy still looks ready to get that rock and try hitting me again.

"I'm as freaked out about how people have changed as you seem to be," I say, slowly lowering my hands. "Please. I'm an EMT and know a lot about this stuff. I can pay you back even for a few days of relief while I get everything worked out."

They both don't know what to do with me. I can't blame them.

"You're an EMT?" the armed girl asks. "The one girl inside is sick. Do you think you could help?" With my year of med-school under my belt, I hope I can.

"I will do what I can," I say. Never make false promises.

"Jocelyn." The armed girl says, extending an open hand to me. I take it.

"Jon." He says, but doesn't hold out his hand. I grab my pack and start to follow them into the cabin.

Jon shuts the door behind me and locks it. Both of the young girls look at me carefully. They are clearly twins.

"Ladies," Jocelyn says, "this is Carter. We had a little bit of a misunderstanding but he can help us. He is a paramedic. Carter this is Sara and Caitlyn." I consider correcting her- I am only an EMT, but I hold it in.

"Delighted. Aren't you both lovely?" The one that Jocelyn said is Caitlyn definitely looks jaundiced. She has already made her way back to the bed before we all take a seat.

I begin to explain my story to them. Then they tell me their own. Jon's demeanor lightens up as an hour passes, and that helps me to feel a little more at ease, as I don't have to stay focused on him. Jocelyn, however, continues to distract me throughout the night. As I searched through the campground I imagined many different sorts of people I may have stumbled upon. She never crossed my mind once. They make me a small meal and feed me as we continue to talk about their plans, and they want to know about mine.

Jon really becomes more amiable when he learns that I know about survival: guns, animals, gardening, and especially medicine. Most of it is a combination of the Boy Scouts in my early days and my love of the Discovery Channel.

After finishing a small meal, Jocelyn and Jon go to the corner and talk quietly. The twins are both sleep at this point. The sick one seems to look even worse. They come back.

"Well," Jon begins, "this may seem sudden, but we would like you to stay with us. You kinda need us now, and we are going to need you soon. None of us have any clue how long this is going to last- but if everything you tell us is true, we have much more to gain with you being around." He reaches out his hand. When I grab it, he pulls me close and lowers his voice. "And I'll be watching you, because if you do one thing to put any of those three in jeopardy – so help me."

"I understand. Thanks Jon." I look to Jocelyn, into her green eyes. She blushes a little. "Thanks to both of you."

It seems I've found a home.

Chapter 21: Sara

I think I like Carter after this past month. Jon says that Carter almost killed Caitlyn when he gave her the wrong medicine at first, but she looks a lot better now. Before Carter came, she'd been getting worse and worse for more than a week.

Besides, Carter's been spending a lot of time with Caitlyn making sure she is getting better as fast as she can. I like sitting with them and talking; he has a lot of good stories from when he was an EMT. He said he'd often get called to this house owned by an old man who had frequent health problems, and no matter how bad the man was when he got there, he'd have a candy bar on the shelf for each member of the attending team.

"The first two times, we didn't accept anything," he said. "Then, about the third or fourth time, he had these caramel peanut bars, and was really insistent. How can you say no to an old man that's on your gurney still wearing an ear-to-ear smile under an oxygen mask? After that, it became habit for us."

He has lots of stories like that. I think the only person that likes them more than Caitlyn and me is Jo, but she won't admit it. I see her looking over her shoulder and smiling as she pretends to read her books while Carter talks. Once she even giggled at a funny part about a story when he stayed at this campground.

"And just then, while we were sitting around the fire arguing over who would take the last strips of bacon from the cooling rack, a raccoon runs up, grabs the two pieces, stands up on its hind legs and gives us a look like this:" Carter held out two clenched fists as if he was holding bacon, tipped his head, shook it, and rolled his eyes. His impersonation of a raccoon was ridiculous.

Jo couldn't help herself. I knew she had been listening, and she giggled with Caitlyn and me. But when Carter turned around, she pointed, "I'm laughing at you, not with you."

She's out hunting again right now. She still hasn't brought anything back, but that won't slow her down. She's said the same thing all week, "I'll get one tomorrow." Then the next day, each time she left, Jon would remind her to be careful, and Carter would glance up at her a few times as she walked into the woods. He has spent some time helping her handle the guns properly. Carter has a little experience.

Jon has been working on basically two things: radishes and archery. He's set up a really make-shift target behind the house just next to his fields. His "target" is more of a tall pile of dirt, and he aims for empty cans that he's jammed into the side after taking out both the bottom and top parts of the cans. He doesn't get the arrows in them very often, but even from far away he hits the mound.

Today, Caitlyn and I are out back with Jon, pretending to write cursive in the dirt with sticks. Really, I want to bother him and Caitlyn wants to watch the bow and arrow. He keeps firing at the piles of dirt in the distance.

"Just another week and we should start to see the plants!" says Jon, pulling the string back for another shot. We hear a muffled "thft" as the arrow embeds itself in the mound, just a few inches from the can most of the way up the side. I continue to bother Jon with all the things that I will try to make with the few things he planted. I have really become good at making stuff up in the kitchen.

THFT. We hear it again. This time, the arrow misses by much more, and on the other side of the can. Jon sighs, and I think I hear him say something under his breath, but I can't make it out. He drops the bow, not seeming to care where it will land, and unstraps the quiver from his back. Without a word, he walks over to his bucket, picks it up, and heads for the lake. I don't think he is improving like he thinks he should.

"Sara, help me!" says Caitlyn, scrambling up and running over to the bow on the ground.

"What are you doing?"

"Help me put this on! I want to try."

"Jon's not gonna like this. He'll be back soon!"

"I just wanna try a few. Let me take some shots, and we'll put everything back just where we found it."

I look toward the trees where Jon went. I can still see him. He doesn't seem to be moving all that fast, so we might have time. "Okay," I finally say, rushing to her side and helping her shoulder the quiver that is only a little too big for her body.

"Ok, go grab the two arrows out of the target for me."

As I bring them back to her, she has already picked up the bow and is finding a way to hold it so that the tip doesn't hit the ground. She's just barely too short for it to be straight up and down.

"Oh well. I'll just tip it a little bit until I... wait! A chair!" She puts the bow down and runs into the cabin. I follow close.

"Caitlyn! Shhh! Carter's sleeping!" I say as we approach the front door. She slows down, and we creep in together to grab the chair.

In no time, we have it out back, and she's standing straight up on the chair with a big smile on her face as she pulls back her first arrow. She struggles to pull it back all the way.

THFT! I'm getting really familiar with the sound. I tried to follow it as it left her hand, but it was too fast.

"Woah!" I can't hold in my amazement. She put the arrow right beside the can! I look up at her, at the mound, and back up at her again. "I'll bet you can't do it again!"

She giggles. "Okay, you're on!" She reaches over her shoulder awkwardly, finally getting her fingers around another arrow. She strings it, pulls it back, and fires again.

THFT! I can't believe it. She put that one right next to the first arrow, except above the can.

She giggles again, just like last time, like she knows something I don't. Reaching back again, she finds an arrow more easily. This time, she strings it much faster, and the draw is much smoother.

"Caitlyn!" we hear, just as she releases the string. I turn to look, and I see Jon, standing with a big surprised mouth as he watches Caitlyn's third arrow stick into the mound, just on the outside of the can.

"Caitlyn, did you shoot all three of those?" asks Jon, putting the pail down next to the rows of planted radishes.

She hesitates. "Uh, I dunno," she says, laying the bow down gently on the ground and fumbling to undo the quiver.

"No no, Caitlyn, I'm not upset," says Jon, picking the bow back up. "Do it again."

"Huh?" she asks.

"Do it again. Put another one in the can."

Caitlyn looks at the target, then Jon, and the target again. She holds out her hand and accepts the bow back from him. He spins her around, pulls an arrow out of the quiver, still on her back, and gives it to her.

"Hold on one second," he commands, hurrying over to the target to pull the three arrows out of the target. "Ok, pull back, but don't release."

Caitlyn does as he asks and holds the arrow by her cheek.

"Ok, that's just how you want your hand, arms, and shoulders to be. Relax the string without shooting." He continues just after she's let the bow come down. "Bring your back foot out to your right just a little bit, and go ahead and shoot again."

She follows his instruction again, and puts her fourth arrow right back in the middle of the can.

"Caitlyn," begins Jon, smiling and turning back from staring at the target for a moment, "that's unbelievable."

"Yeah, you're weird," I chime in.

"I've been watching you closely," she says to Jon, ignoring me.

We spend the rest of the day practicing. When Carter wakes up, we put on a show for him, and then a repeat performance when Jo gets home from hunting, still empty handed. She's really impressed with Caitlyn, but it's easy to see she's frustrated, too.

"I'm going to start dinner," she says, sighing. Jon made something awful last night and we are just going to have him clean up from now on.

"I'll help!" I jump up and scamper to her side. Watching Caitlyn shoot was fun for a little bit, but I'm bored just watching now.

Jo smiles. We walk around the house, past Carter who's now working on building some sort of outside oven on the side opposite the pump.

"Two of my favorite three girls. Soon I should have this working and we can try baking something." he says, looking almost at us.

"And how many girls do you know these days?" Jo asks, coyly.

"Not important," Carter responds, smiling. "So when are you going to bring back an animal so we can cook it in this thing?"

"You see, that's my problem. I keep going out there thinking, 'I've nowhere to properly cook a deer if I actually kill it.' Maybe if you'd hurry up and finish, I'd be able to move past that."

"Consider it done. You'll need one tomorrow then." He raises his eyes and continues working.

We round the front corner of the house and head inside.

"How about..." begins Jo, trailing off as she thinks of what's in the pantry, "canned green beans and some cheese over rice?"

"We had that last week."

"And we're probably going to have it at least once a week all winter."

"Oh."

"Because of the whole having to live in the woods thing," she says jokingly with a wry smile across her face, "still working on that."

I laugh a little bit. "What do I do?"

"Go fill up this pot for me!"

The meal comes together quickly and easily. It's just a matter of stirring the rice, and pouring on some cheese sauce that I add a little bit of my own special touch to. After boiling the canned vegetables, we're ready to serve it.

"We make a good team" Jo says, turning to me as we serve up the plates.

I like the sound of that. I'll make sure we don't have rice and broccoli over and over again when its her turn.

Jo opens the door and yells, "Dinner's ready!"

Chapter 22: Caitlyn

"Breakfast is ready, Caitlyn. Wake up!" I try to pull the covers over my head, but Jo's hand is sitting on my shoulder keeping me from getting the sheets all the way up. She laughs and grabs them. "Come on! Get up! Eat with everyone, and if you'd like, you can go back to sleep."

I think about that for a little bit, and even though I'm still fighting her, it actually sounds kind of good. I open my eyes and see Sara stumbling over to the table.

"Last day of muffins!" says Jon, pulling them out of the pantry. I stop fighting against Jo's pulls on my sheets, but I only let her pull them back slowly. The past few mornings have been cold. Winter is here. As soon as they're past my knee and I still haven't felt that chill, I push them all the way off and roll up onto my feet.

"It's not as cold today," I say slowly. My lips don't want to move yet.

"Yep. It actually looks really nice outside. Hopefully the deer will think so, too."

I just stumble over to the table and peel open the pack of mini muffins. I liked muffins a lot, but a few weeks straight of these little pastries is a little annoying. Sometimes we make bigger breakfasts and other times we just have these packaged foods. I don't mind too much that they'll be gone after today.

"Are you two going to practice again today?" asks Sara, looking at Jon and me. She's talking slowly, too.

"Sure. I don't think I can read any more of that book without sprouting leaves, anyway. Besides, trying to plant anything is in the past." he replies. It is December.

The only person that hasn't said anything yet is Carter. He's not really a morning person. It's not like he's mean. He just quietly pops his mini muffins, one whole one at a time, into his mouth and washes them down with some coffee that he found in a neighboring cabin one day. In front of him is the police radio. During the morning and evening every few days he turns it on and scans for any messages. A little static emits from the speaker. He turns it off and seems to think about what he'll do all day. This past week, he'd started to make tools out of branches, rope from bark, and stones that he'd found. The tools seem pointless, especially in Jon's opinion, but it keeps us busy. I got a chance to help him a little. I liked it when he said, "Caitlyn, bring me more brope." I try to absorb everything he knows.

As we all finished breakfast, I still felt good about going back to sleep, so I crawled back under the covers and closed my eyes. I start dreaming again almost immediately.

My dreams are cut short, though. The echo of a distant, loud boom rouses me. It's just loud enough to wake me up, but faint enough that I have to think about whether I actually heard it or not. I get up and look outside, and Sara comes with me. Jon said we would practice, so maybe he was working on the target.

We see him looking up to the hills, and by the time I bundle up and get outside, Carter is walking around the house to meet them, too. His feet crunch over the light layer of snow.

"Did you guys hear that?" he asks.

We all nod, and I rub my eyes. After a moment, Jon goes back to working on the target so I follow him. Sara helps Carter with his next project, which looks like it will be some benches for the fire pit that he finished a while ago. Jon and Carter both have leery looks on their faces from the gun shots. I have become good at reading faces

About twenty minutes later, Jo comes running out of the woods with the rifle in tow and a huge smile on her face. "Carter! I hope that oven's finally ready to be christened." she says, really excited. "Come with me!"

Another twenty minutes go by as we all hike through the woods to find Jo's first kill: a small white-tailed deer. I look up to see everyone's' reactions. Jo is still smiling, still thinking of how proud she is that she's finally gotten a deer.

Jon and Carter look puzzled, though. "So... now what?" asks Jon looking at all of us in turn.

Jo squints a little bit and turns to him. "What do you mean, 'What now?' You guys kinda just..." she trails off.

"We do what?" asks Carter.

"You know. Get the meat out."

Carter and Jon look at each other uncomfortably.

Jon starts. "Well, you've dissected a lot of things, right? Med school? Biology? Stuff like that?"

"Well, yes, but never with the goal of figuring out where a good cut of steak is."

"But you can figure it out, right?"

Carter sighs and shakes his head out of disbelief, not disagreement. "I could really use a cigarette right now." He pauses. I walk over to the deer and roll it over a little bit.

"Are you sure it's dead?" I ask.

I kneel down next to it and put my hand in front of its nose. It's not breathing, and I can't hear anything in its chest. "I think it's dead." I feel kind of bad for it.

"If worse comes to worse," says Jon, stepping toward the deer, "I'll bet the concept of a rack of ribs goes for a deer as much as a cow." He squats down, hoists the deer over his shoulders, and heads back in the direction of the cabin. "Paging Dr. Carter," he yells over his shoulder, "your patient is ready to see you now."

The four of us follow Jon down the hill and through the trees. All of a sudden, I'm kind of excited to have something new to eat. The boys seem hesitant, and I almost offer to cut up the deer. I look at its open eyes hanging over John's back. I bet I could figure it out.

About halfway back, Jo breaks the silence. "So I saw something very strange while I was hiding high in the hills this morning." We all look at her at the same time, and she takes a moment to make eye contact with each of us. "I saw a vulture nest in one of the dead trees at the top of that hill," she continues, pointing behind us and to our left.

"Well, that's pretty low for a nest." says Carter, apparently listening intently.

"I wouldn't know," replies Jo. "But the thing that caught me off guard about it was, well…"

"What?" I ask, wondering what made the nest so strange.

"I think one of the baby vultures was eating another."

None of us know exactly what to say to that.

"That's really gross," says Sara, settling on something obvious.

"Why would that happen?" I ask.

"It's actually not too strange," adds Carter. His claim surprises all of us. "Fratricide is common. If the young go without food or needs provided by the family for long, they often rely entirely on instinct. And instinct isn't always... pleasant. And it never turns out well for the weakest even if it includes siblings."

Jo still looks confused. "I just don't understand how it benefits them at all. I mean, doesn't that mean that in difficult times, the number of vultures gets even smaller?"

"Yes, but the vultures that survive will be much more likely to make it in the long run because they were able to sustain themselves while they were young. That's why that part of animal instinct hasn't died out. We might see it as barbaric, but some animals do whatever it takes to live."

By the time he's finished talking about the vultures, we're back at the cabin, and Jon has laid down the deer and is looking at it with his hands on his hips. "I guess we just have to give it a shot. Let's get started," he says to Carter.

Carter pulls two different sized knives out of his pack and hands one to Jon. "Jo, can you take the girls inside, please?" he asks. Carter told me one day he would teach me how to gut an animal, when he has it figured out. I have my doubts.

Later, the three of us come back outside just as the sun is setting. Apparently Jon and Carter did something right.

They're sitting across the oven from each other, rotating most of the deer over a low, but hot fire while some of it cooks in the oven itself. I think it's the first time I've seen them smile at each other.

However, I feel like I have missed out.

Chapter 23: Sara

"What would you like, Jon?" I ask, sitting across the table from him. I thought I kind of liked Carter before, now I knew he was a great addition. He found a way to dry the pelts from Jo's hunting, and we have some extra little blankets to keep us warm. With as cold as each day gets, the extra warmth was great for us. Our saw hasn't had any rest in a while, so we always have a fire going in the cabin. Jon is always outside finding more wood for us and keeping me warm all the time. All things considered, we're warm and healthy. The only problem is that we're really bored.

I want to change that though, and with Christmas coming up quickly, I think everyone would feel much better if they have some presents to look forward to. "So what is it? What would you like?"

Jon is breathing deeply over a steaming cup of coffee, blinking and thinking.

"I know what he wants," says Caitlyn. She walks over to him, and croons her neck forward so that she can look in his eyes. "Hmmm..." she says. "I think you want... a tree-house!"

Carter laughs at this. "Did you read that in his mind?"

"Uh-huh," my sister replies.

"Caitlyn, we like to call that projection. In reality, you want a tree-house so you can work on shooting arrows from up high, but since it's Jon's turn to pick, you want to believe that he wants it, too."

"No. Jon wants a tree-house, so we can hunt from it." she says firmly, frowning at Carter.

Now Jon laughs. "I've made my decision, and I would like a tree-house."

"Really? Yay!" exclaims Caitlyn, turning back to Jon.

He shakes his head. "No, I'm just kidding." Caitlyn's head sinks. "Anything? How about some chocolate. Or at least some fruit."

"Oh my gosh," continues Jo. "A chocolate banana split sundae? I'd die for one."

"So you're telling me in the middle of a cold winter, for Christmas, you would like a cold dessert?" asks Carter, half through a chuckle. "Well we already have the fireplace and blankets, but to complete my Christmas wish, we'd need a TV. I used to love watching movies at night next to the fireplace with my family."

"Ok Caitlyn, now it's your turn. What would you like for Christmas?"

Caitlyn tries to purse her lips, but the smile that she's holding back comes through. "A tree-house."

Jon almost spits his coffee out from how quickly his laughter erupts. I think I'm laughing more at his face than I am at my sister.

"Well I would like a puppy," I say after the chuckles have died down. "Even just to pet for a little bit. That's what I'd want for Christmas this year."

As everyone sits around the table dreaming about other things that Christmas might have brought them this year, I decide that these presents need to happen. The tree-house is easy enough. Carter just has to build one. Maybe Jon will help

Carter. They have gotten along this week. I need to think about the other ones some more.

Carter stands up and stretches. He must be going back outside to light a fire and maybe do some more work on what started as a fire pit and oven has several benches and tables. If he keeps working on it like this, it'll have a roof by the time spring comes around. Now is a good a time as any to see if he'll help me with my Christmas ideas.

"Where are you going?" I ask cheerfully.

"Just outside. I think the only thing that would be better than being able to roast these deer and rabbits would be if we could roast them inside. If I can get that oven covered it will make some of the cooking easier."

"I'll help!"

He smiles. "Well you'd better get bundled up! We might be out there for a while."

I hurry to gather my jacket and a scarf. Without gloves, we've just been wrapping my hands in towels or others' scarves and making sure a fire is always going. Between Carter and Jon, we always have a good supply of wood.

While lashing some more tripods together next to the fire pit, already blazing, I start my sales pitch. "So what is your next project going to be?"

He sits for a minute, and looks around the side property for a moment. "I'm not sure," he concludes. "Maybe I'll build a shed. We could get some of the clutter out of the cabin itself."

"What if… we built a tree house for Caitlyn instead?"

"What?" he asks while laughing. "I'm sorry, I don't mean to laugh. But you're serious, huh?"

"Yeah! Why not?"

He pauses again, this time, tipping his head and raising his brow at the end. "You're right. We don't have long till Christmas so it'll be more of a platform, but sure, why not? "

"Really? Great!" That was easier than I thought. "Well, I'm kind of thinking that we should try to make everyone's gift happen. Can you help me?"

"I'll tell you what, let me look at my calendar to see if I have any pressing appointments." Carter mimes an agenda in his hand and scanned through an imaginary calendar. With a shake of the head, he closes his imaginary book, and he looks back up at me. "Well, I'm clear until January. Let's brainstorm while we finish the little spit!"

While we strip some knobs off of some straight, thick branches, we talk about what everyone had mentioned and come up with suitable substitutes for their presents. I'm just waiting for when Carter will ask what I'm going to do for his present; I don't have an answer yet.

"The tree-house is easy enough. Jon and I can put one together, even if it's rudimentary," he says glancing between random points in the air as he thinks. "The chocolate, however, will be much more difficult. What did Jon say? At least some fruit?"

"Uh-huh," I say, with a proud smile creeping across my face. "I know exactly what to do. Caitlyn and I found some berries on a walk with Jo a few weeks ago."

"Oh did you? What kind of berries?" asks Carter with a little suspicion.

"Let's go look! It's not far." Just a few minutes later, Carter and I are inspecting the bush that Jo, Cait, and I had found near the end of one of our walks.

"Aha! Do you know what these are?"

"No…"

"These are elderberries. They're everywhere, they're edible, and," he pauses to pop one in his mouth, "they're delicious."

I smile. We found Jon's present. "Can I try one?"

"Sure. Have a few." Carter pulls a small stem of the berries off of the plant and hands it to me.

"Now what about Jocelyn?" I ask as I pull my first elderberry off of the twig.

"Well, if you let me use some of these, I'll take care of that. In the meantime, I'm going to teach you how to carve so you can make a bowl for Jon's present."

We hurry home and finish the second cooking spit. Carter also enlists Jon's help with the tree-house. He never asked about his present...

This will be the tricky part. I have to get the other three to help me with a skit for Carter without them thinking about their own gifts. I just have to avoid the subject of Christmas.

While the boys are out wood-working, I get Jocelyn and Caitlyn to sit down.

"Ok," I begin, clasping my hands together. "Remember when he said he used to watch movies with his family in front of the fireplace? We should surprise him one night and put on a play for him!"

"Aren't you thoughtful?" says Jo, smiling. "Let's do it." Caitlyn does not look as excited.

Well that was much easier than I thought it would be, too. Now I just have to make sure that the skit is ready around whenever we celebrate Christmas.

* * *

"Wake up, Sara. Guess what day it is?" Jo gently shakes my shoulder. It doesn't take long for my drowsy brain to figure out the answer to her question. Instantly, I'm grinning ear to ear and shooting up in bed.

"MERRY CHRISTMAS, EVERYONE!" I yell. I hop out of bed and skip around the room with Caitlyn in my wake. She's this excited and she doesn't even know about her present yet. She hasn't acted this giddy in a while. The third time we lap the room, we stop in front of the calendar that Jon carved and wait for him to move the nail from December twenty-fourth to the twenty-fifth.

"Jon, can we show her?" I ask.

Jon smiles and looks at Carter, who is also smiling. "Sure! But we have something for you first."

I stop hopping around and look at everyone. They're all looking at me with big smiles, too. "What's going on?"

Carter answers. "We didn't want you to be left out of all the gift giving. Everyone get warm. We're going outside."

Oh no, did they all figure out what their presents are? I'm a little nervous as I put on my jacket and scarf and pull my blanket off the bed. I'm the last to go outside.

The minute I look up once I'm out the door my grin comes right back. Our front yard has four different snow-sculptures of puppies.

"They're so cute!" I yell. I jump to the nearest one and look right in its eyes, and I extend my hand to pet him. He has two different sized acorns as eyes, and a piece of rope around his neck for a collar. Each time I pet him, a few flakes of snow come with my hand and blow in the gentle gusts. They must have woken up late last night and done this.

"Thank you all so much!" I don't know how to express how grateful I am. For the first time, I realize how much I love them all.

"Ok, my turn!" says Caitlyn, with bursting anticipation. "Jon, you said you had something for me, right?"

Jon laughs. "I did. We have to take a little walk though. Come with me."

As we walk into the trees, I jump onto Jon's back and he carries me up the slope. Jo starts singing "Winter Wonderland," and Carter joins in. Soon, we're all singing, and I turn around to look at everyone's faces. The only thing that seems out of place is how Jon keeps looking back and forth between Jo and Carter. It was no secret that those two have spent a lot of time together. Jon still wasn't sure about it and there had been some arguments.

"...but as long as you love me so..."

"Alright, alright, a new one," says Jon, bringing the carol to an abrupt halt. "Frosty, the Snowman..." he starts, and we all follow suit. I could tell Carter was a little irritated.

The tree-house isn't that far into the woods, and we approach it quickly. As it comes into view, Caitlyn's excitement and astonishment comes on, but slowly.

"No..." she begins. "You guys didn't! Yay!" Her enthusiasm turns into a shriek of glee. I jump off Jon's back and I run with her over to the foot of the host tree where a few rungs of thick sticks lead to the first platform. There are only two medium-sized platforms and only one has a roof of any sort, but Jon and Carter did an amazing job.

For a moment, as Caitlyn and I play, I feel like I'm back in our old living room, pretending to be running around a castle. I look back and see Jon watching us. On his face, there's a new kind of smile: a genuine smile that I don't think I've seen yet. It's my favorite one. Behind him, Carter and Jo are throwing snowballs at each other. One connects, and it startles Jon out of his pleasant daydream.

"Alright, alright, that's enough of that," he says, turning around slowly.

Carter is still laughing. "Okay. It's time for your present anyway."

"My present?" asks Jon, surprised.

"Yep. And yours, too," replies Carter, addressing Jo.

"Really?" asks Jo, with a pleasant grin spreading across her face.

I can't wait to surprise Carter after these, and my anticipation makes the walk home seem even faster than the walk to the tree-house.

"This is for you," I say to Jon, having poured a can of frozen elderberries into the wooden bowl that I carved.

"And this is for you," adds Carter as he hands a cup to Jo. He had poured elderberry juice into a cup that he fashioned and filled with snow. It's no sundae, but it is a cold, fruity dessert.

Both of them take their first bites and close their eyes, savoring the flavors that were at least near something that they've been craving for a month. They hold those bites in their mouths for a really, really long time, and when they open their eyes again, they look at each other with the most serene smiles.

"Now for you Carter," I say. I wink at Jo and Caitlyn. We take him and Jon inside, sit them down on the floor with blankets next to the warm fire, and start our play.

We are going to survive this winter.

Chapter 24: Jocelyn

Jon had championed this past meal with more success from his garden. He made a stir-fry in a batch of oil that Carter had extracted from our soy beans. I'm grateful, because the meal tasted like heaven. I scrape the last of the carrot peels into the fire and finish stacking the plates. Tomorrow, I have to cook, and our short list of recipes jumps through my mind.

This summer has been good so far and as I look out the window and see Jon, Carter, and the girls, I begin to think that we could live like this forever. It has been nearly nine months since we first stepped into this cabin. I don't think I want to, but I know we can survive here ten more. I grab *A Tale of Two Cities* and lie face up on the bed. I plan to use the last bit of sunlight finishing my book. I finish a page, but I soon feel my foot being shaken. I look up and see Carter at the foot of my bed.

"Hey, let's go for a walk." Usually I relish any time with Carter, but I'm really looking forward to doing some nothing. We work so hard during the summer day and to simply sit and read is ecstasy. I fold the corner of the page and put it on the bed between my legs.

"Fine." I exhale with a smile.

We start to walk along the path headed to the lake. Jon gives a small wave to us and then continues helping Caitlin aim at a haystack with a bull's-eye painted on it. She already has three arrows in the center. Caitlin has really mastered archery and Jon is doing his best to make her the best she can be. I think she is teaching him a few things as well. Sara still seems hesitant about the prospect of hunting animals, so instead she just wants to talk Jon's ear off. Her infatuation with him has grown a lot these months. It makes the three of us smile.

Carter leads me further along until we are down by the lake. The sun is setting and we won't have too much time out here. Jon doesn't like wasting batteries if we don't have to. He's right of course.

A log looks perfectly placed besides the lake. We both have a seat, and I look over into his brown eyes. I can't help but get lost in them sometimes. Ever since he came out of nowhere in the fall, I couldn't imagine life without him.

He looks back at me. "What is the tension sometimes between you and your brother? When things get too serious you become distant. I understand his and my tension, but not yours."

"It's been like that for a few years." I try to avoid a direct response. "And actually you haven't seen the worst of it. It's a long story."

"Good thing we have a half an hour before the sun goes down. Luckily, I have no upcoming appointments."

There's no way around it. Carter should know anyway. I bite my lip and begin:

"It was almost three years ago. I was thirteen at the time. He was a bit more outgoing, to say the least, than I was in high school. He went out many times with his friends and stumbled in a drunken mess occasionally. Mom and I usually covered for him as best we could with dad whenever this happened. Dad would have killed him. Then mom pretty much blackmailed him into driving me to gymnastics and everything else. In retrospect, I guess we should have tried more to stop it. Mom thought he would get sick and learn a lifelong lesson. Well the lesson came, but it wasn't because he got sick."

Should I even be telling this story at all? I look back at Carter, and he's sitting there, attentive. Leaning forward with his elbows on his knees and his hands folded. He's blinking infrequently, and patiently. I can't just stop now.

"It was around two in the morning and he still wasn't home one Friday night and he wasn't answering his phone. Mom and I were out looking for him, worried; I had refused to go to bed until my mom did. We had no luck at his usual spots in the park and decided to just wait at home. As we were pulling into the driveway, they hit us. His friend's pickup truck crushed our small white compact. His friend, who shouldn't have been driving, slammed into the driver's side of the vehicle. Glass shattered; steel twisted. My mom was pinned and bleeding badly, and I was covered in glass but mostly okay. I saw my brother stumble out of the passenger's side of the car. He screamed and then ran inside the house."

I pause for a moment, remembering what that panic felt like.

"Dad heard the crash and was running outside. He worked early on weekends so he had been in bed at 8. On his way out he saw Jon curled in a ball and crying. My dad asked him if he was okay. The shame on my brother's face and the stench of alcohol answered my father. I know the look he gave still haunts Jon. My father ran outside and pulled me out of the car and tried his best to help mom. He stayed with her until the firefighters showed up. She…she died while they were trying to get her out."

I feel my eyes slowly water. I have thought about that day a lot over the past few years. It should be commonplace to me by now. "Needless to say, our family's relationship with my brother has been strained ever since. Jon has tried everyday to make up for what he did, but that is not something that is easily made up."

Carter finally spoke, "My God, I can't imagine…"

"That's not the end of it either, I guess. Three days after that I found him in his room with a gun on his lap. I have no idea where he had gotten the silver revolver but I still shake when I think of the image. Beside him was a note. I was able to talk him down and took the gun off of him. He has been weird about guns ever since, because I think he was going to do it. If I wouldn't have gone into his room to look for any more pictures of mom, I think he really would have shot himself."

Carter nods.

"I took the gun to the police station and said I found it in the park. This didn't endear me to him any more than the last event. He became less my brother and more a nuisance that must be put up with daily. But he tried so hard everyday, especially with my dad. He never touched alcohol anymore and aside from a few after school activities he never had a social life. Jon devoted himself to make either his sister's or dad's lives better in anyway. He was going to sacrifice himself for the rest of his life. I found it in me to slowly forgive him, but dad never forgot. So when the plague came, one small relief was the assurance that Jon would always be there, he knows nothing else by now. He would give his life just so I don't feel sadness."

We sit in silence for a few seconds and then Carter adds, "We may not get along, but we have that in common."

"What do you have in common?" I responded, looking up at him. I notice that he looks nervous. He's working his fingers together and keeps looking down at them.

"We both would die for you." Carter looked ahead as the sun reflected over the pond. I put my head on his shoulder and grab his hand. I look up to see him looking right back at me.

I stretch my neck forward. Our lips meet, and my body feels warm all over.

Chapter 25: Sara

"Turn that down." I yell out of instinct. It sounds like someone left a TV on and that static fills the cabin. My eyes widen as I realize what I am saying.

A muffled voice joins with the static. I sit up straight to see Carter already in front of his radio. He turns it on every sunset and sunrise to check the emergency bands. We thought he was crazy. Boy, were we wrong.

Carter picks up the radio and begins to slowly tune it. It alternates between clear and fuzzy until Carter finally stops it on a station. In a heartbeat the five of us gather around the small speaker. I don't think one of us is breathing.

"This is an emergency signal to the Ohio River Valley. The UN Relief and Relocation program will have a station established at the Trinity Shopping complex on August fifteenth and expects to be operational for six months. Please report to this facility immediately. This is an emergency signal to the ..."

Before it sets in, Jon picks my sister and me up in a huge embrace and is shaking us right to left in his arms. A giant smile stretches across his face. Carter and Jo hold onto each other and then they join us and all of us embrace for the first time.

"Does this mean things are going back to normal?" Caitlyn asks. For a second I almost think she's worried she will have to leave her forest, but then the excitement lights up her face. Carter runs to his pack and pulls out a map.

"Now, if I remember correctly that is right at this intersection." He points to the map as Jo leans over and checks.

"That's exactly where it is," Jo exclaims. She embraces his arm and their eyes lock for a second. I may be young, but I know those two have something going on. It makes me happy. I grab Jon's arm tighter and he looks down at me with a smile.

"So when should we get going?" Jon looks at Carter and Jo. The two quickly separate.

"Let's spend today getting everything ready and then head out in the morning. It's still a day's drive and we are going to have to stop for fuel," Carter directs. He takes a few deep breaths and his grin diminishes. He quiets his voice, "We also need to consider that this may not work out. We should hide everything we have here in case we need to come back. We don't want someone else to come along and take everything we worked so hard for and have problems on our hands."

That doesn't seem necessary to me, yet I spend the next four hours putting all of our tools and equipment into containers and then burying them in the woods. Jon tries to convince Caitlyn that she should leave the bow, but she demands to take it. She can be so silly sometimes. We won't be hunting for food anymore where we are going. As Jo and I are burying the last of the pots and marking them with some sturdy sticks, we hear yelling coming from the cabin. I start to walk toward it but Jo puts a hand on my shoulder.

"Stay here for a sec.," she says. "It's Jon and Carter, you know how they get."

"You said like fire and dynamite?" I respond. Jo laughs.

"Yea."

Those two have had trouble getting along. Sometimes they seem like best friends in front of me, but when we're gone, they are at each other like snakes. I don't understand it. Jo gets tired of it, but usually it's over such small things that she tells us not to worry at all. She laughs about one of them being the "alpha male."

Boys are so stupid.

By the time I come back to the cabin, everything seems resolved. We have a canned dinner since everything we need to cook is hidden away. It reminds me of the first dinner we had here. Sometimes I thought things were going to be bad, but they turned out alright. When we celebrated Caitlyn's and my birthday in February, I could not believe the feast those three created. However, Jon and Carter were really worried about this winter coming up. Last year when winter came, we had a lot more food from the grocery store, and even then we were hungry a lot. Now we're down to almost nothing in the reserves.

At dinner, we talk about things we hope they will have wherever they relocate us.

"Alright, I'll start this out." Carter jumps in. "I hope they have some video games. It's been forever since I went all ninja." Carter karate chops the air in front of Caitlyn while making a slap sound through his lips.

"Figures," Jocelyn begins. "Call me shallow, but I wouldn't mind spending a week shopping for new clothes. Granted we don't have any money at the moment, but as soon as I get new credit card, I'm maxing it out."

Caitlyn joined in, "I am going with her."

I look down at my outfit as she says this. The five of us have worn basically the same things for months. Sure we do a good job of washing them but they are starting to look pretty beat up. After a lot of hesitation and a few arguments, Jon and Carter finally went to a department store when the temperature got dangerously low in January. They found some stuff that fit Caitlyn and me, despite the fact that the store was mostly empty, but now we are growing and need another trip. I guess we have grown at least four inches since we arrived here. Caitlyn is now taller than me.

"Fried food." Jon admitted. I feel my mouth salivate. Real flavor has been rare here.

"...School..." I force out. They all laugh. I do miss it. We finish our food and soon find our way to the beds. I usually try to think of mom and dad before bed, but it is getting harder and harder. When I think of family, everyone here comes to mind. I want to spend the rest of my life with Jo, Carter, Caitlyn, and most of all Jon. I drift to sleep.

* * *

"I didn't want to have to spend a night out here." Jon exclaims. "This wrong turn killed us."

"If we keep going we can be there by 2 or 3 AM," Jo adds in.

"It's too dangerous at night. Besides, we have been on the road all day. We're tired, and we don't know what awaits us at this place," Carter observes. The three of them continue to discuss our course of action as the SUV keeps traveling down the road. Caitlyn and I just stare out the window. We got off to a little bit of a late start this morning, and the journey has been anything but smooth. The highlights? Siphoning for gas and traveling a few miles in the wrong direction – twice. We are going to arrive at the UN relocation center much, much later. However, no matter what happens, my family will keep me safe. I smile at the back of Jon's head.

Carter points ahead and taps Jon with his other hand. "Wait, what's that?"

I press my head against the glass. We're driving through a wooded and relatively hilly area, and it seems like some modest houses were built along the side of this route. Up ahead is a series of turned over cars in front of one of these buildings. Several boys are standing around, and one is waving his hands over his head. It has been a long time since I have seen anyone else. As we get closer I can tell he is smiling. He is wearing a clean navy blue jacket, like what my dad wore to work, and he even had a red tie. He must be around the same age as Jocelyn. Carter shuffles in his seat. She puts her hand behind her, to the gun she usually carries in her belt.

"They look like they want me to stop. What do you think guys?" Jon asks us. He looks nervous. "I can floor the pedal and blaze past them."

Carter squints his eyes at the boy. "He looks harmless enough and I can see both his hands. Those other boys are what I'm worried about." A few boys dressed the same stand in front of a boarded up house. "See what they want, but if I tell you to gas it, gas it."

"Carter, I don't know the last time Jo and I did this we..." Jon responds.

"Stop," Jo says. "He looks like a schoolboy. Maybe they need help. Show them some humanity."

I can see Jon struggle to obey them. The SUV comes to a halt and the waving boy comes up to Jon's side. Jon rolls down the window.

"Can I help you with something?" Jon asks sternly.

"Hey, how you all doing?" the boy replies, not really answering Jon's question. He looks into the car and smiles at each of us. Especially Jo. "It's more the other way. Is there a way we can help you?"

"Why the kindness?" Carter inquires.

"Sorry for my rudeness, sir. I am a representative from the Sanctuary. This is one of our outposts."

"What the hell is the Sanctuary?" Jo asks leaning forward between the boys.

"Basically we are people that have made the best of this world. We want for nothing and welcome anyone we can into our home. The more the merrier is our philosophy, especially if the more includes beautiful ladies like each of you." He gives Jo and me a wink. She blushes, and I am pretty sure I do, too. Carter and Jon look uneasy. "But seriously you five, I imagine you are headed to that UN center up ahead."

"How do you know about that?" Carter shoots back at him.

"We have people checking frequencies night and day to see if others are in need. Also you are not the first car to pass us with that destination. Most people this week pass us a lot earlier in the day than you. Nonetheless, you still have a lot of travel ahead of you, and it will be dark in an hour or two. We turned an old motel into our home, and I guess it's still kinda used as a motel. You all would be welcome to spend the night. The past few nights, we have been a haven to those traveling to the aid and relocation center."

"What's the catch?" Jon asks. Carter nods with him.

"None. I promise. We have made a very successful life and know children and teens like us are really struggling out there. It's why we call it the Sanctuary, because we want to help all of the people we can. Our car is heading back in a few moments and you can just follow us there. You all look like you could use a good night's sleep."

"Why aren't you all headed to the UN center?" Caitlyn asks.

"Well, it may seem hard to believe, but many of us have found purpose out here. We aren't ready to leave this world just yet." Caitlyn nods back, she seems to understand him. I don't know why anyone would choose this way of life when they could go back to the old way!

The boy continues, "It's just fifteen minutes down the road. Through that neighborhood. It's up to you."

"Give us a minute" Jon informs him.

"Alright well we are going to load up here in a moment. You can choose to follow us or not. Either way, I wish you all the best." He smiles and walks away.

We talk it over, and we settle on following them. They tell Caitlyn and me if things get bad to keep our heads down as we get out. Their car leads us through a neighborhood and up ahead we see the Sanctuary. It is a sight.

Chapter 26: Jonathon

Over the entrance to the motel is a large banner that says, "Sanctuary." The large motel is centrally located and has a brick wall that partially surrounds the main building. It looks like they've added in a few flipped cars and some barbed wire to make it more secure. I turn to the twins and can tell that they feel unsure. From the outside, this place looks like a jail. Although keeping people out is pretty similar to keeping them in.

I pull the SUV into a parking space beside the car that led us in. I see a few dozen boys come out of various rooms and approach us. Obviously new people cause a bit of excitement around here. The older boy who I talked to walks over to the office. The rest of the boys don't seem to know what to make of us. As we get out of the car, our original host returns with someone. It does not take much effort to tell that this was the man in charge. He looks to be just about my age. His brown hair is long and parted to the sides of his forehead. His attire matches the navy blue and red of the others. He has a smile of confidence that I would hate to be on the wrong side of at any time. He extends his hand to me.

"Jon." I say with my outstretched hand.

"Jon?" the boy checks. "Call me Saul. Glad to meet you. Welcome, Welcome. I'm glad my boys found ya'll out there. You are going to come to find this is quite an establishment my boys and I have made here." His eyes go up and down each of us. I can tell he was taking us all in. Saul motions with his right hand and the group of us begin to walk around the perimeter. The fence around the building is very extensive. Floodlights are mounted all over the complex and wooden watch towers have been constructed on every corner. Safety will not be an issue here.

"Thanks for you and your boys' kindness, sir. The road is dangerous and this is definitely better than spending a night out there alone."

"Why are there no girls here?" Caitlyn jumps into the conversation. Saul lets out a slight laugh and looks down at her.

"Well, ya see, young lady, all the boys you see around here, we all used to go to the same all-boys school. When the plague struck, the school started to take in students as parents began to die. Our numbers grew and grew and soon, we students were the only ones left. One night the school caught fire and we had to relocate. Surprisingly this motel was deserted so we made a home of it. I'm sure you know how dangerous it is out there, so we reinforced it and armed ourselves. A bus full of people took advantage of us once and we were not going to let that happen again." Saul taps the side of the holster on his hip and winks at me. "We have prospered here. We have a garden in the back, and there is a secluded farm a mile in the woods where we keep some livestock. We also have patrols that scrounge for supplies. The Sanctuary gives its residents the best quality of life in America – or so I have heard."

"So why has no one joined you?" Carter responds. He looks suspicious of Saul. Saul just grins back at him.

"Many have come and stayed but they want to go on. Some continued the search for their families and others for the border. Recently people have had hopes about that UN center you all mentioned to my boys earlier. So recently we decided to call this place the Sanctuary because people seem to seek us out for temporary security on a journey. It is a safe place and I hope others will think about staying and not just passing though – as long as they can help out of course!" he grins at me. The five of us will definitely be able to earn our keep here. I smile and nod back.

He takes us on a complete tour. There is a shed filled with generators and they have nearly the whole place wired with lights for the night. Containers of gasoline are safely stored in several drums just outside. Saul says they have enough gas to last almost six months, but they still go out daily to get more. He says a few of his intelligent boys are even working on finding and installing solar panels for the roof.

The swimming pool is now a receptacle to collect and store freshwater. In the back they have a boy who spends the whole day sterilizing water for them to drink. Along with that they still managed to find a way to keep the bathrooms working. All of our faces light up when we hear that. In the office, he shows us their food supply. They have boxes and boxes of canned goods. Saul advises me that those are for emergencies. They prefer to use food from the gardens and farms if at all possible.

He tells me many meals involve eggs and potatoes – but his chefs are finding ways to always make them taste different. Saul assures me that this Thanksgiving they will be having three turkeys. He tells us that we missed dinner, but he will gather the odds and ends that were left of the meal to hold us over until breakfast. His cooks will apparently have an especially large breakfast for us in the morning.

I'm truly astonished by his Sanctuary. The food, the generators, and safety. It's an amazing accomplishment. I don't know why people would leave. That UN center seems like a good idea, but this seems to be a better one. It's the only certain thing.

After the complete tour they show us to our room.

"Let me know if you need anything Johnny-boy." Saul says as he walks away. I don't care for the name, but I won't bring it up. He's just shown me that there are havens of humanity despite the crumbling of civilization.

The room is on the second floor, right above where the car is parked.

"I had this room prepared specially for you during your tour. I hope you enjoy the accommodations!" Saul says.

One of the boys helps with our luggage. They go to grab Carter's bag and Carter quickly pulls it from his hand. He can be a jerk.

Saul opens the door for us and gives me the key. He turns to me and Jo, but he seemed much more focused on her. "Lights out is at eight-thirty tonight. We don't like to use more of the generators than we have to. We advise you to stay in your rooms. It can be pretty dangerous around here in the dark. Last week I fell and had a lump on my head the size of a baseball." He laughed to himself and rubbed the back of his head.

"Thanks." I respond.

"Thanks!" the twins nearly yell at him in unison. They look incredibly happy as they run and jump on one of the one queen beds. Much nicer than our typical arrangements on the wooden bunks. It looks like Saul has arranged four beds into the one room. We were lucky that we found him today. The sun is beginning to set as I shut the door to the outside.

Tomorrow Carter and I can go check out the UN place while the girls stay here, safely. On the slim chance that the UN place doesn't work out, we may be able to make a life here. The cabin worked, but to be in a community again feels amazing. To interact with new people and new ideas... it makes me feel different. Human.

Everyone changes and lies down on the beds. The day has been long in the crammed car. My fingers interlock behind my head on the bed and I stare at the dark ceiling. I laugh for a second. It seems that someone had decorated the ceiling with little glow in the dark space stickers. I get everyone else to look at the ceiling and we all laugh. Carter begins to tell the twins the background of a few of the constellations on the ceiling.

"You see, ladies, people believed that when heroes died, the gods would immortalize them in the stars."

"Is Superman up there?" Sara asks. She gets a laugh out of Carter.

"Well no, Superman wasn't Greek." Carter responds.

"How do you know Carter?" Jo asks him with a sly look.

I make eye contact with Jo and I smile back in the dark. "Jo-Jo, I'm pretty sure Superman is an alien."

"Well then obviously he is already up there!" Caitlyn exclaims. We all laugh. Even Carter and I share a grin. He begins to tell the twins about the gods and goddesses of the past. He has their complete attention. I wouldn't admit it, but he has my attention, too.

And for once, even more so than last Christmas, all of us are happy. We have nothing to worry about, not even in the back of our minds, in the walls of the Sanctuary.

Chapter 27: Carter

I can't sleep in the bed they give me. The bed is soft and comfortable, or I guess what I used to consider comfortable. Now, it is a distant feeling that makes me uneasy. I swing my feet to the side and push myself up with my arms. Everyone has fallen asleep already. It's been a few hours now. Jon is in a bed beside mine. He is sound asleep. The twins are sharing a queen bed and look completely peaceful. Jocelyn, well, she looks perfect. I never get tired of waking up before her and seeing her asleep.

I go out to the front wall and look out the window. The compound is completely dark. It makes sense to have an eight-thirty curfew; those generators need gasoline and it's best to save them for other priorities. They advised us not to go out at night. "It wasn't safe," he said – too dark. I figure I'll take my chances with these people and open the door into the night air.

Really, they did do an admirable job turning the motel into this safe haven. All of the rooms, the wall, the farms, and the utilities make the compound a feat of engineering and society that probably exceeds anything that the youth of the country have achieved in the past year. The cars that they've flipped and the barbed wire especially add to the security. But I also feel trapped.

Something about this place rubs me wrong. I'm not sure why yet. Why would people not stay at this place?

I walk to the fence perimeter and gaze at the trees which are barely lit by the crescent moon. Some parts of the fence are chain-link and others are brick.

I exhale. If I had a cigarette I would light it. Luckily, I ran out a few months after the plague and managed to prevent myself from finding more. It was a nasty habit. I defy anyone to go through a pre-med program at my age and avoid all vices. I cling my fingers to the fence and breathe deeply. Maybe this place won't be too bad.

A muffled scream comes somewhere from the compound. Was it a scream? Maybe some boys are messing around. I start to walk back to the motel building.

I hear it again, and it stops me dead in my tracks.

There's no mistaking it: a young girl's scream. I start to run toward the other end of the complex. The scream sounds like it's coming from a room on the other side, far from our room. I race through the darkness and come out along the other face of the building. I clench my fist and prepare to take someone's head off. As I turn the corner I see a group of the boys. Many of them were about the compound throughout the day. I instantly dive down behind a dark vending machine along the building.

A half dozen of them are standing along the wall between me and the room from which I think the scream came. Some of them have lanterns and a few of them seem to be coming from that room's door. I remember it from the tour earlier. Saul said that it is the workout room. Each of the boys carries a machine gun on his shoulder. Where did they get those? They are laughing and carrying on. One holds a brown bottle – two guesses to what's inside it.

The muffled scream rings out again. It is definitely a girl, and it is definitely coming from the "workout room."

They told us that Jocelyn, Caitlyn, and Sara were the only girls on the compound. They lied. I peer out to get a better look at the room. The curtains are shut, but white light shines through. I squint trying to get a better glimpse.

The door opens and light pours into the parking lot, blinding me for a moment. I withdraw my head slightly but keep looking out. A figure comes through the door. The farther it gets, the more I can make it out. It is a girl no more than fifteen. Her shirt is ripped and hangs off her left shoulder. Her nose bleeds into her mouth.

Some of the boys start to laugh. One grabs her around the waist. She resists, and he throws her to the ground in response. She pushes herself up and slowly walks a few doors down and goes into another room. What the hell is going on?

Then I see him. Saul walks out of the same room. His hands are fixing his belt, and he laughs.

Before I can comprehend it I'm running as fast as I can back to the room. I trip and scrape my knee along the ground, but it doesn't slow me down a second. I throw the door to our room open and it slams into the wall. Everyone jumps in their beds.

"Carter, what in hell are you doing?" Jon asks. His right hand holds him up as his left hand rubs his eye.

"Jon, guys, we need to get out of here now." I close the door quietly behind me. I take Jocelyn and Jon into the bathroom and tell them everything I saw. Jon looks furious. Jocelyn looks like she might throw up.

"We can leave tonight. The car's right outside," Jon starts. He leans out the bathroom door. "Girls get your things together we are leaving in five minutes."

"Why?" Sara asks. Caitlyn on the other hand is already up and throwing her few things together.

"Please just do it," Jocelyn asks sweetly. She does a better job with the girls than Jon when there is stress.

I turn to Jon. I feel the disbelief on my face. "Jon, we can't just leave. There is that girl. She needs us."

Jon looks at the floor and then his eyes meet mine. "I feel bad about it, but getting these three out of here is my first concern." He walks past me and grab's Jocelyn's bag. He pulls out the revolver and puts it in the back of his belt. It's the first time I've seen Jon hold a gun. We can't leave that girl. I grab his shoulder.

"We're not leaving her. She may not even be the only one." I tell him, nearly pleading. Jon grabs my hand and throws it off my shoulder. I look at him in disgust. I have seen so many people since the plague that had forgotten what being human meant; I didn't think Jon would be one of them.

"We are leaving now." Jon replies and he slams against my shoulder as he walks past. I can't believe him. Jocelyn stares at both of us. She wants to help me, but she will side with Jon. Needless to say I cannot blame either of them. It doesn't matter. Right is right. I walk to the bed and reach under the bed for my bag. I pull out my pistol, check the barrel, and tuck it into the holster along my back. I shove another clip into my front pocket.

"Fine Jon, get them out of here. I'm staying." He nods, acknowledging my resolve.

Jocelyn comes up with an idea, "Jon if you're so worried we can take the girls out and then we can come back after this girl."

"No, they may hear or see the car. It's not a risk I'm willing to take. This discussion is over," Jon definitively answers.

We silently head out the door and I help them pack up. Jocelyn gets in the passenger's side door. "Please get in Carter," she begs. I shut the door behind her. Jon looks over and gives me a dirty look. He turns the car on and they drive out without turning the headlights on. I watch as the red from the brake lights slowly drifts off. As they head out of the entrance I hear the yells of the boys. They see them. Now is my chance.

After running to the building, I press my back against the wall and slide around the corner to make my way to the front. I peer over to the room I saw the girl go into. Then men are distracted by the SUV. They don't know what to make of it. I continue around to the door. Closer. Closer.

My eyes become blinded and I squint. The facility's lights have been turned on.

If any of them simply turn around, they will see me. I nearly run to the girl's door. The boys are still distracted by the entrance. Some seem to even be running after it. One boy is within ten feet. I reach for the bronze door handle and pull it down. I push the door open, go inside, and shut it. The security latch is missing.

I turn around. A small table lamp illuminates the room and I see her squatting in the corner. Her arms bend in front of her face and her back pressed against the wall. She looks dirty, her clothes are torn, and she shakes. She may not even be fifteen.

"Please, not again." her blue eyes quiver between spread fingers.

"Shhhh, no honey, it's okay. I'm here to help." I hold my hands up in front of me open-palmed. She looks at me with uncertainty. She doesn't trust me, and I can't blame her. "I just arrived here earlier today and I was hiding outside and saw when you left the work-out room. I'm gonna get you out of here." Her defense breaks down and instantly her arms are around me and she is crying into my chest. I hold her tight. Damn Jon for leaving. She releases me and sits on the bed.

"What's your name?" I ask

"Tina," she answers. "I came here a few weeks ago with my two cousins. They were all nice to us, then after a while they separated us and started this. They are both dead..." her voice breaks.

"Tina, you are going to be alright, but we have to leave now. They are all distracted outside. It may be our only chance." I reply. I reach into by holster and pull out my pistol. "By the way, my name is Carter." I put a round in the chamber.

I look out the window, lifting up the curtain with my left hand. Several of the boys are now missing and the others seem distracted. They seem to be paying little attention to this room. Then it darkens. The lights are out. They've shut down the generators again. I grab Tina's hand and slowly open the door. If we go around the other side, we may be able to make it out the exit. Once we get off of the property, we can quickly disappear in the woods.

We slide along the building. I use what little light the stars give me to search for any weak spots in the fence. The bricks, chain-links and barbed wire make it impossible to get out. The entrance is the only way. We make it to the other side and the only sounds are the boys still yelling. It will be a sprint to the entrance. We can make it.

"Can you run Tina?" I ask. She nods. She looks uncertain, but I sense the hope she feels that she has not felt in probably a long time. "Hang on."

I grab her with my left hand and grip the gun in my right. We accelerate to a run, and close quickly on the entrance. They don't see us. I hear the patter of our feet against the black pavement. Just twenty feet left.

Fifteen feet.

Ten feet. Almost there.

The lights in the compound come back on around us. Behind us I hear yells. We can still make it.

"Just give up Carter." A voice says... in front of us. We come to a halt. Saul walks into the light from the entrance. I begin to raise my gun but the two boys beside him already have their rifles pointed. Instead I use my left hand to pull Tina behind me and drop the gun to the ground. The two boys move close to me with their guns inches from my chest. I guess this is how I die. Saul opens his mouth. I wish I could ignore him.

"Nice try. Well not really. Tina, go back to your room. I will deal with you later." I feel her start to drift away from me. I turn my head she is backing up slowly. Then she starts to run. She runs to the entrance. To freedom.

"No, don't..." I reach out with my hand. Just as she's about to make it through the fence, the air explodes as gunshots fill the motel lot. She falls. My chest tightens. How could they do this? "Saul I'll kill you, you son of a..."

"Carter, enough. You are going to be laying beside her in a moment, boy." My teeth clench. Saul walks up to her body and flips her over with his foot. I want to kill him. I want to kill him so badly. He looks at me with a grin. I feel my eyes widen and I grin, too. He sneers at me, "Finally seeing the humor in this all?"

I answer, "Yea. Look to your right."

Saul turns as he hears the unmistakable click of a revolver hammer snapping into its armed position, and looks directly down the barrel of a Smith and Wesson pointed at his skull.

Jon came back.

Chapter 28: Jonathon

All the other boys turn toward me. The barrel of my gun shakes slightly as it hovers inches from Saul's head. The whole place is lit up like a stage from the floodlights on the dark rooftops that cover the Sanctuary. Most of the boys are gathered around the main motel building, but some stand against the second floor railing with their guns pointed at, well, me. There must be about twenty of them. The two boys on the ground that just had their barrels against Carter's chest take a few steps back. They look scared, and they don't seem to know whether to aim at me or Carter. I hope I'm not advertising my fear as much as they are, because I'm pretty sure I feel at least that scared.

Saul's body provides pretty good cover; none of them have a shot. At least I hope, anyway. I nod to Carter and glance for a second at the girl's corpse. Their spotlights make the small blood pool look like shattered red glass against the black pavement. It's my fault. I had to choose her or Jo and the twins. Those three will always be my choice, and I can't regret. I hate Carter for making me come back to this. If we would have just left I wouldn't be here.

I wouldn't have to face the girl who I so readily left behind.

"Saul, tell your boys to stand down and let Carter leave with me. There is no point in this going any further. I don't want anyone else hurt." I calmly say to Saul while my heart beats through my chest. My glance returns to the girl on the ground. How could I sacrifice her without a second thought? I want to run away. I want to find a corner in a room and pretend that she isn't dead and that this didn't happen.

Like the last time. I want to escape this feeling just like the last time my decisions accidentally killed.

The thoughts drain from my mind. No. I will never do that again. I clench my jaw and tighten my grip on the handle of the gun. No, never. I remember the boy in the supermarket.

This is the same. My gun moves closer and rests against the back of Saul's head, twisting the back of his collar in my other fist. I turn toward the pair close by. "You boys back off." I bark at them.

They seem to hesitate. Their eyes squint down the sights, but soon they begin to relax and bring their muzzles down and take a few steps back. Their feet scrape further backwards. Carter picks up his fallen gun and stands beside me, putting Saul between him and all of their guns. I want to punch him. Not now.

I drag Saul backwards by his collar, farther from the threshold of the Sanctuary. He looks over his shoulder, his left eye finds mine. "Come on, Johnny, there is no need for this. We were just having fun. It was Carter that ruined it." Saul's profile lets out a grin evoking a deep, hateful glare from Carter's eyes. My hand pulls Saul back farther and farther. I raise my gun toward the motel.

"Now all of you stay back. If any of you come after us we will finish him. Come collect him in one hour along one of those houses down the street, but if I see a damn flashlight moving down the road a second sooner his brain will be splattered all over the road." That was violent; I hope this works. "Do I make myself perfectly clear?" My roar echoes throughout the compound.

Nobody speaks. My response comes in the form of Saul's comrades lowering their guns and backing up further.

We are soon hidden by their makeshift wall and I grab Saul by the hair and begin running for the nearby houses a few hundred yards down the highway. Carter turns and kicks the gate shut, and catches up to us down the road Saul tries to hold us up a few times, but Carter helps drag him farther. A few punches to the kidneys dissuade him from struggling. Over my shoulder, I see the light of the Sanctuary get smaller and smaller. The gate remains shut. A few yells come from inside, but I think they are going to listen. Our feet slap against the still road in the silence of the night. We go in between a few houses surrounded by bushes and trees. Somewhere private.

"The car is a little up ahead; pulled behind the third house – that green one. I told the girls to wait fifteen minutes and if I wasn't back to leave without me." I pause for a second with my words. I catch my breath and glare at Carter, "I didn't want to come back for you. Jo made me." I raise my voice to him. "You put them ALL in danger!" I throw Saul into the bricks of the house and bury my finger into Carter's chest. Maybe now I'll hit him.

"I couldn't leave that girl," Carter answers. Surprisingly, he is not angry. He seems to nearly be pleading for me to understand. I do understand. Carter made the hard choice and I made the right choice. Those girls need to come first, and if he isn't going to...

Saul starts laughing. "She was pretty worn anyway..." There is a blur where Carter just was.

Carter's fist buries itself into Saul's stomach. I have never seen so much rage in his dark eyes before. Saul buckles to the ground and Carter brings his knee into Saul's nose. Saul falls back and lands sitting upright. His smile is no longer there as blood oozes from his nostrils, but he still manages his confident smile. Saul clenches handfuls of grass around. He hurts, even if his face won't show it.

"How long have you been doing this to her you-?" Carter swears at Saul while striking him in the face. "Who the hell do you think you are?" Another punch. I look away briefly into the back yard. A swing gently rocks in the front yard of the one house in the night air. Saul screams something. Carter stops.

Saul spits up some blood. His dirt and grass-stained hand wipes his mouth, smearing the blood down his chin. He stares atCarter, the right side of his mouth grins. He begins:

"A few months back we gave refuge to this whole school bus full of girls – some gymnastics team at a national competition when the virus struck. They were headed to that damn UN place all you travelers talk about, but they were about out of gas and starving to death." Saul's eyes move between us, his voice peppered with madness. His grin grows and more blood bubbles between his words. "We gave them everything. We kept them alive. And what the hell did we get in return? Nothing. After a week, they smiled and waved and left. I was sick of being taken advantage of by damn women my entire life. We managed to make this perfect society without a single woman. We only knew one good use for them. So we swore to ourselves that the next group we helped we would take our thank you anyway we damn well pleased." His bleeding grin returned after this statement. He's an animal. "We've had that girl back there for three weeks. Too bad her cousins didn't make it that long."

Carter's rage built up beyond his control and again he was on top of Saul, punching him over and over. After a few moments, I gather myself and pull Carter off of him. Saul spits up more blood. His grin is gone.

"What did you want with us?" Carter snarls at him.

"My boys are to give the 'Sanctuary story' to any one who passes by with a girl who we think may be worth our while. Imagine my boy's surprise when you rolled up with three. Some terrible tragedy would have befallen you two in the next few days and then... well you know." Carter back handed him across the face. Saul's eye is swelling shut.

"Carter we have to get moving. They could already be looking for us in the darkness. I don't want to be in a fight." Carter looks like he has calmed down. I start to walk away. We need to get out of here-get back to the girls.

"Just one more thing, Jon." Carter pulls back the hammer on his gun and points it at Saul's head. Even that warped confidence is gone from Saul's face as the silver steel presses again his forehead. Carter looks to me; I nod. Never before had I wanted someone to die so badly. I stare at the back of Saul's head waiting for the bullet to come through.

Then I hear Sara's voice from behind us.

"You guys are safe! Come on the car is out front. Jocelyn saw you guys come back here and pulled up. Let's get... Carter what are you doing?" She must have finally seen Saul before us. I quickly turn and bend down and tell her to leave, but her eyes are already filled with horror. "What are you two doing?" A tear is forming in her eye.

Carter's hand shakes with the gun, and he brings it down. He has always been tough, but he isn't an executioner. I am, but Saul is broken and harmless to us at this point, anyway.

"You're not worth it." Carter says, spitting at Saul's feet. He puts the gun away in his belt and picks up Sara before walking to the car. Sara stares at me over his shoulder all the way around the house. I am left with Saul.

"She saved your life." I turn and start to follow them.

"Sorry it ended like this Johnny, I was really looking forward to getting to know that sister of yours." Saul is up on his knees when I turn around. My hand brings my revolver back to his head. My finger tightens on the trigger. With Darry, part of me wanted to do it. Now, all of me wants to do it. What's more, I know I can.

No. I exhale, rather frustrated. Not with the girls right next door. The little humanity I have left holds back my finger.

I flip the weapon in my hand and whip the pistol as hard as I can into the side of his head. One of Saul's bloodied front teeth flies against the brick wall. He drops. I leave him.

I walk around the house and see the SUV in front. The twins are in the backseat and Jo is behind the wheel. She looks anxious. Carter shuts the door to the backseat and walks toward me on the front lawn.

"Jon I'm sorry. I know that didn't go well and..." My fingers form a fist, but I don't use it.

"Carter, I want you out of here. You put all three of them in danger and you knew we couldn't just leave you. You knew Jo would never allow that," I whisper into his ear. "I want you to tell the girls that you will be leaving us at the next stop. That you just wanted to get us this far and have other things to tend to and will meet up with us later."

"Jon I think you are overreacting..."

"No Carter, you are leaving." He looks at me defeated. I almost feel bad. "I don't know what the rest of this road will bring us but I can handle it without you. I don't need a hero, just someone who will put those three above everything else."

"Jon, we are almost to the UN center."

"I don't care if we are fifteen minutes away. I want you out. This incident just shows that anything can still happen. We last track of what the world turned into while we were in the cabin."

"Fine." Carter's emotion surprisingly vanishes and he responds coldly. "I'll find my own way."

The girls want to know what happened and Carter manages an abridged version of the events. When it comes to the girl he tried to save, he tells them that she went her own way. I think the twins buy it. The two of us don't share any words until we find some abandoned cars.

As we siphon for gas, Carter explains that he must leave. I don't even completely understand the story he makes up. The twins get a little upset. Sara cries. Jo handles it just as poorly, and glares at me. She knows why this is happening, and no matter what words she uses, Carter continues to do what I ask. Jo puts up a fight, but after a half hour Carter is finally gone.

Jo is going to hate me for a while. It's best for us.

In another time, I would have given my life for that girl, her fallen body flashes again in front of me. Now though, it's different. We can't save everyone and it's dangerous to be around someone that thinks we can.

I will sacrifice anyone and kill anyone who endangers these three.

Chapter 29: Caitlyn

I pretend not to know what is going on. If Jon and Jo knew that I'm aware of all of it, they might try to talk to me about it or something. I don't need that. I'm not a stupid child. I understand.

I know what those boys were doing to girls back there in the Sanctuary. It doesn't take a genius to put together the words I overheard when Carter explained it to them in the bathroom.

I know Carter left because he didn't listen to Jon and put us all in danger. His "searching for a friend" excuse may have fooled Sara, but that was it. I will keep playing along.

Carter headed off in some hot-wired blue car at the gas station. I think I will miss him. He gave us a strength I will miss. His car flew into the distance while we all loaded back into the SUV. Sara's and Jo's eyes are still red from their tears. I just shut the door and stare out the window. Jon gets in the driver's side and we return to our goal – getting to the UN center. We have around a half a day ahead of us according to him.

We drive along and pass the outpost where the Sanctuary boy first waved us down. Several flipped over cars in front of a house make a pretty good station. I think I would do a few things differently. The hill on the other side of the road really makes it hard for them to see if anyone is coming up. I could even sneak up that hill. I press my forehead against the glass and peer down the slope as Jon guides us around the now abandoned station. Below are more houses and streets. It reminds me of where Sara and I once lived. I look over to Sara and give her a smile. She struggles to give one back and continues to pick at the bottom of her blue shirt.

We drive for hours until the sun beams straight down.

"We have maybe two hours of travel left. Let's stop for a few minutes to stretch," suggests Jon. The rest area is tucked away among the trees and looks vacant. He needs to stop for a few. I would keep driving. That's probably what Carter did. The SUV pulls along the side of the road and Jon and Jo immediately get out. They didn't share a single word the entire trip. They both fade into some nearby trees and I make out the shouts of their argument. Usually I try to listen, but I know what it's about. Who wouldn't? I climb out of the back seat and walk over to a picnic table. Some names are carved into the wood, along with some hearts and a few random designs. I run my fingers along one of the cuts. When were these markings made and how different of a world was it then?

"What are they yelling about?" Sara comes up to me and asks. She sits on the bench and holds her hands in front of her.

"I'm not sure," I lie. "They are probably just upset that Carter didn't tell us that he was planning on leaving us so suddenly."

"I can't believe he did that to us." Sara looks sad and she tilts her head down. I sit closer to her, our shoulders touching. "I mean, we don't have much farther, right?"

"No. We don't. This will be over soon. Carter will meet up with us later. Why don't you go lie down in back and try to sleep?" She nods and disappears into the car.

I look down the road. The shadows of the trees stretch across it, leaving the whole highway in shade. I pull my pen knife from my pocket and begin sharpening a nearby stick to take up my time. The shavings form into a pile on top of the picnic table. I have it notched into a pretty sharp stake when Jo walks out from the woods; Jon comes out several paces behind her. He stops at the SUV and leans against the hood. Jo keeps walking a ways down the road and sits on the guardrail. I throw the stick back onto the grass and join her.

"You okay?" I ask.

"Yea. I will be glad when this world is behind us." She answers. I don't agree. Jon turns to us from the car just a few dozen feet away.

"We had better get going," he yells to us.

"Give me a few more minutes before I wanna be next you again," she yells. She gets up and starts to walk along a path that leads into the forest.

"Where you going?" I question.

"I can see a stream down there. I'm gonna splash my face with some water and then we can get going." She starts to head into the woods. I sit at the base of a tree and watch her slowly escape my view. A few birds land in the grass a few feet away, and they peck into the grass. One stares at me and then up into the sky. My eyes look up too and squint when they meet the sun's rays. Closing my eyes, I breathe in the air.

Being out here feels right. It feels like home.

Between everything I learned from Jon and Carter, I could survive out here. It would not be hard at all. I would be away from all of this...this nonsense. Sara isn't cut out for this though. She needs to be somewhere safe first; then we will see.

The birds suddenly fly away. It startles me for a second, and one even seems to catch my hair as it flies by. Looking down into the path, I can make out the stream but Jo is nowhere in sight.

"Jo?" I say rising to my feet and beginning to walk down the path. "Jo? Jocelyn?" I accelerate to a run, and soon my feet touch the side of the creek. She is nowhere to be seen. "Jo?" I get louder, cupping my hands around my mouth.

Where did she run off to? Why are girls so hysterical?

I follow the creek around the bend. Then I see her.

Well, I see them.

Three of the Sanctuary boys are quickly walking to the back of a car. The one in the middle has her slung over his shoulder. Instantly, I duck behind a bush and watch as they throw her into a trunk. All of them get into the car except one. His gaze peers around.

Saul.

He is soon back in the car and it takes off along the dusty trail. I want to run back to Jon, but I hesitate. I freeze. Fear grips me. That monster, Saul: he… he scares me. My left hand shakes. What Carter said they – he – did… I imagine Jo. I imagine Sara.

I imagine me.

A few seconds pass, but it feel like minutes, and I sprint back to the campsite. My legs take me as fast as they possibly can up the dirt trail. My toes catch a root and I fall.

Jon and Sara hear me stumble. Both of them can already tell something is wrong and they meet me halfway.

No one will scare me like that again.

Chapter 30: Jocelyn

My head smacks into something metal and my eyes shoot open. I see a few moments of light, a blurry face, and then the trunk slams shut. My screams are muffled by the metal and the roar of an engine as it comes to life. The car seems to take off down the road as I bounce around the trunk. My hands struggle to find a latch of some sort, but they are bound by some rope and I am face down against the carpet. I am trapped.

Wait, I am trapped. They've captured me. I remember now; I was hit on the head when I was at the creek. I start to scream louder and louder. My feet pound into the steel, the backseat, anything. It takes a few moments but I calm down. The abrasive carpet hurts my face and the kicking isn't helping.

The Sanctuary's boys weren't hard to identify with their navy blue coats. I hope they didn't get anyone else.

Walking away from Jon was a mistake. Sara wasn't far. I hope she hid. My wrists rub back and forth, trying to undo the rope. I soon give up and try to lower my pulse. They have me and there is nothing I can do about it right now.

I think several hours pass as I bounce around, keeping claustrophobia at bay.

Suddenly, daylight pours into the trunk. As my eyes focus I see a few of the boys who once greeted us into the Sanctuary. Their expressions are now much different. They grab me by my shoulders. We are at the outpost where we first met them. They drag me past the turned over cars and into the house. Boys with rifles follow the ones dragging me. I would struggle, but even if I could break free it would still be worthless. My feet drag across the threshold of the front door and they slam me into a chair. I soon find my bonds attached to the back of it. Surprisingly, they leave me alone.

The ropes hold my hands together and the bandanna in my mouth restricts the scream that is trying to escape my throat. I cough. I try to shake lose. Worthless. Accepting defeat is not always that easy. I look down at my clothes. They are covered in dirt, probably like my face and the rest of me. We were so close to the relocation center.

If Jon wouldn't have flipped out on Carter this wouldn't have...

The door to the room swings open and Saul is standing there. A pistol is holstered to his hip and he seems dressed in new, clean clothes. He gives me a smile. There's a hole where one of his front teeth had been. He probably has Jon or Carter to thank for that. Probably Carter. Jon doesn't have the strength to really hurt anyone.

"Surprised we managed to find you so quickly?" He says. I grunt through the gag in my mouth. I don't care. I need to get out of here. "My boys had been tracking you since the second you left our little home. Jon was pretty naive to think he could get away so cleanly from us. Within an hour of you all leaving me I was packed up in a car and blazing down the road to get a little payback."

He pulls another chair away from the wall, flips it around, and sits down on it, leaning forward against its back.

"I was a little worried we would never catch up to you. But then there you were, sitting along the side of the road. You made it easy when you decided to wander down a little further.

Too bad that little one didn't come with you. We would have liked to have her, too."

With all my strength I try to pull my hands loose from the back of the chair. I yell through the gag. The rope does not give way. I collapse back into the chair. Saul moves closer. He licks his upper lip and looks me over.

"Man was I pissed when I thought I lost you, but now that I have you back, I can take what is mine." His hands go down my body. My feet struggle to free themselves, but they are also lashed together. Struggling against the rope seems pointless, but I keep trying. This can't happen. He steps back.

"I imagine that coward of a brother and your boyfriend will be here soon. Guessing their type they will be here within the hour without a plan or preparation. When we are finished here I will pull you up against a window and maybe you will be lucky enough to watch them die." He puts his hands on his hips confidently. I shut my eyes for a second. He is right. Jon will come in here raising hell the best he can. He'll be determined, but he won't get far. And Carter. Carter is probably already enjoying it at the UN station, sitting back and waiting for us to roll up and hoping Jon will have calmed down.

Saul leans in close. He presses his lips against mine. I bite as hard as I can into the bandana and try to turn away. He grabs the sides of my head and forces me toward his. I struggle. He punches the side of my head. The force knocks me and the chair to the ground. My head slams into the hardwood floor. I taste blood.

With my head against the floor, I look up. I try to struggle, but the rope is still tight. His hand moves along his gun holster. I imagine the girl Carter tried to save at the compound. That would be me soon. I feel a tear stream down my eye.

BANG.

A gun shot. Then, another one.

Saul stands upright alarmed. "Boys, what the hell is going on?" He looks down at me. "Well that was sooner than I expected."

He grabs me and with alarming strength, pulls both me and the chair upright.

"You hold tight for one second."

Please Jon. Don't kill yourself.

Chapter 31: Sara

I have never seen Jon look like this. He almost scares me as he tells us to get in the car.

"Jon we will get her back." I say.

"They took her. Those..." he swears a lot, but I understand. I guess they followed us all the way out here. They must have been pretty mad at Jon. I never was completely clear why we had to leave, but Jo pretty much got the point across to Caitlyn and me. Those men were bad people, and we had to run away from them.

Houses fly past us as our car goes down the road. Caitlyn speaks up, "Jon, what are you going to do?"

"They are going to stop at their outpost house, I am sure of it. They know I'm coming and don't want to take a chance of ruining their damn Sanctuary. This road will take us to the neighborhood right beneath that house. I can probably sneak up the hill and take her back." Before we left the park, he pulled out one of Carter's maps and figured out our path. The flash of anger goes across his eyes again. I don't like this Jon.

I answer him. "I wish Carter was here." He looks at me. He sees my face and his anger seems to fade. I think he saw that he needed to calm down.

"Me too." he responds. He continues to accelerate. Some hours later Jon brings the car to a halt, few words are shared between us. We're near the top of a hill, and we pull off. Jon asks Caitlyn for the binoculars and jumps out to the front of the car.

"Do you see anything, Jon?" I ask shouting out the window.

"Yea they are there alright." The road we are on eventually leads directly to the outpost itself. However there is a set of houses at the bottom of a hill in front of the outpost. I guess he could try to sneak up the hill and then across the road. It doesn't seem very safe.

"Jon I don't think this is..."

"I have to, Sara." He looks straight at me. "There's no other way." He takes the car out of park and he backtracks until he comes to the bottom road. He chooses a driveway and pulls in. Reaching down, he pops the trunk and walks to the back, leaving the keys for me. I can hear him rummaging through our supplies in the back.

"Sara, wait fifteen minutes, then I want you to take Caitlyn and head to the UN center. Caitlyn, you remember how to drive and read a map right?" She peers out from above the backseat. She nods. Certainty is in her eyes. Jon pulls out the revolver from the pack, pauses for a moment, and then tucks it behind him in his belt. It is the first time I see him hold a gun from when he first found us. Then, he grabs the ranger's shotgun. We hid the rifle in the cabin. He goes to shut the trunk but pauses again.

"Although you may not understand how right now, you girls made me feel like I did more right in this world than wrong. You gave me worth. You are my family"

I grab his right side as he shuts the trunk and a moment later Caitlyn has joined us.

"Don't leave us." I whimper. Caitlyn pulls me off of him.

"He will be back soon." Caitlyn tells me. Jon rubs the top of my head.

"I will." He looks sad as he turns and head up the hill. I fall to my knees. I grab my sister and feel the tears pouring from my eyes. He means everything to me. I scream out to him but I don't think he hears me.

He was my Prince Charming.

Chapter 32: Jonathon

Leaving those girls was one of the hardest things I've ever had to do. But my sister is in danger right now. They can manage. Caitlin especially has become strong. I climb steadily, weaving from tree to tree with my eyes focused at the top of the hill. The outpost is just over the hill and across the road. When I reach the apex, I slide behind one of the destroyed cars they've used as a road block. There are two boys on the front lawn, but I have no idea how many more are on the inside. Both of them have rifles at the ready.

One in the chamber, four in the stock. I remember from Carter's crash course a few months ago. The revolver in my belt has five shots. I move up behind another broken down car, remaining hunched over. I've managed to surprise them it seems.

Through my rising and falling chest, I feel my heart pounding. It's so strong that it pulses up into my neck and head. This is it.

I turn and rest my gun on the car hood and aim at the closer boy. I line up the sights right over his chest and pull the stock to my shoulder. Any hatred I have for guns is gone, and I would use anything to save her, from a frying pan to a shotgun. The boy has a gun, and I know he would kill me without a moment's hesitation. That poor girl flashes in my mind, and my transformation is complete. I will do anything to save those I love.

I pull the trigger and brace for the recoil. The first shot misses but shatters the window behind him. I adjust and fire again. The pellets tear through his body. He falls as I turn to the other sentry.

The other boy starts to shoot. His aim is awful. He is young, probably ten. I almost feel bad. Almost. I pump and pull the trigger. It hits him in the arm and also shatters another window in the house. He begins to scream. That doesn't stop him though. He keeps shooting at me. Saul has these kids trained to die. I see other boys start to peer out the windows and some begin shooting.

I fire the last two shells and the young boy finally starts screaming. I throw the shotgun to the side and grab the small revolver. It looks the same as the gun I had in my hand so many years ago. The boys open fire. They have assault rifles and I brace myself.

So this is what the world has become.

Bullets continue to tear through the other side of the car. The small explosions and ricochets cement my feet tighter to the ground and I press as close as I can to the driver's side door. Every muscle in my body aches, but I know that I cannot give up here. She needs me. More than that, I promised my dad I would keep her safe. But most of all, I swore to myself that I would never let anything happen to her, no matter what it took. A bullet shatters through the window above me and showers me with glass. I reach to my neck and swipe the shards away, cutting both my neck and hand in the process. Warm blood runs down my spine and I see a puncture on my left hand. Red droplets fall to the street.

If I don't move now, they are going to kill me.

I glance behind me to where the twins are hiding over the hill. I imagine they are still as I left them, huddled together with tears in their eyes. When I had first charged into the fray, they screamed at me to stop, and their screams continued for a while, but were barely audible when I went over the hill. Any noises from them would be completely gone amidst the chaos.

Could they have been found already? Probably not. They are safe from these monsters' bullets on the other side of the hill. I am the one in danger. My sister is the one in danger.

Mustering up the courage, I quickly peer through the shattered glass toward the shooters. There are at least six boys in the house. Two were behind a make-shift barricade of wood and brick on the front lawn and the others were peering out the house's already shattered windows. At least three of them have guns. I duck down just as another bullet embeds itself into the car's steel. They have me pinned down, and my only small hope is their need to reload. I use my bloodied hand to recheck the cylinder in my own gun. It only holds five shots, my only five shots, and it is not nearly enough. They have bigger guns. Most of all, I would be lucky enough to even hit the house with this thing.

I hate guns again.

A portion of the tire to my left is torn away by another flying bullet. What's left of the tire deflates and the car crashes down to the hubcap. I really hate guns.

The gunfire all of a sudden ceases. An eerie silence spreads over the lawn. My ears still ring from the noise of bullets, and the boys are shouting amongst themselves. I look up and notice all of the boys staring back at me. They have stopped firing, but my heart continues to the rhythm of the gunshots. What are they doing? Then I hear *his* voice. His rusty tone seems to echo off the asphalt street and stirs my insides. To think I trusted him.

"Is that really you ole' Johnny boy? Well if you want her this bad, I guess I could offer a trade."

I grit my teeth for a moment and yell back, "What do you want Saul?"

"I know you still got those two other girls. Send them this way and I will give you back your precious sister. She's got a bit too much fight in her anyway." His words reek with a confidence that sickens me. My father was right; humanity is gone.

"Go to hell." He is never going to take the twins, and he knew damn well that I am not going to give them up. His laughter responds to my demand.

"Come on Johnny, it's not that bad of a trade. Besides, we wouldn't dream of laying a finger on either of those girls. I mean not for at least another year." He truly is a monster. I glance over the hood and see the teeth of his smile. One of the front ones is knocked out, just the way I last left him. He is laughing. The boys to his left and right have moved closer to me. I am trapped. A small pool continues to grow on the asphalt as drops of blood from the cut on my neck run down my arm and off my revolver. It will probably turn from a pool to a pond soon. He yells again, "Tick-tock, tick-tock."

Bang.

A shot fires into the car. He is getting impatient. A few of the boys are laughing at me. I have one option. I stand up and look him in the eye.

They look at me and they look shocked.

Chapter 33: Jocelyn

No matter how hard I try, I can't free my hands from the back of the wooden chair. Jon is right outside, and he is going to get himself slaughtered. I need to get out of here. I can barely make out his yells with Saul. What is he doing? I try to scream but the damp bandana muffles my voice to barely a whimper. My eyes wander around the floor. There has to be a way out. Outside of my desolate room I can see a few of the boys peering out of open and shattered windows. They pay no attention to me tied to the chair.

Then I see a knife in my peripherals. One of them must be behind me. The knife slashes downwards.

I shut my eyes and bite the bandana as hard as I can.

Chapter 34: Sara

I hold my sister as tight as I can. How could Jon have left us? I can't lose him. I didn't mind the gun shots earlier because then I guessed he was still alive. Now it is quiet, and I may have to tell Caitlyn that we need to run. Jon gave me the car keys, but Caitlyn can barely see over the wheel. We could run; there has to be help in one of the houses around here. I release my sister and leave the car. I search the houses behind us with my eyes. We would be better off hiding than trying to run away. Jon? How could he do this? I turn to where my sister had been, but she is not in the driver's seat anymore. I freak out and glance all around. How can she be gone?

I see her just as she goes over the hill with her bow in hand.

Chapter 35: Jonathon

Getting up on my feet, I see three on the lawn and six in the house. All have their guns pointed at me. Big guns. I make a mental note as I look Saul head on. I would be kidding myself if I thought that I could take them all out. I walk around to the other side of the car and set my revolver down on the asphalt.

"This doesn't have to happen, Saul. You're not a monster. Over this past year, you've just been trying to protect your family. That's been your first goal: protect them. And you were betrayed and you want payback. I'm just trying to protect my family, Saul, and they did not betray you. Give her back and we can just go our separate ways." I try to plead with what little hope I have. "If not, some of us, maybe all of us will die.

Right here, right now." He starts to walk toward me, slowly. "Just give me my sister." Maybe... just maybe.

Saul takes larger, more confident steps now. He stops in front of me. In his left hand is a pistol, still focused on the center of my chest. I prepare to humiliate myself.

"Please Saul, I'm begging you, here." I drop my small revolver to the ground. "I am sorry for what happened in the Sanctuary. Imagine if you had a sister. Would you allow all that to happen to someone you love?" He looks me up and down, eyebrows furled. "Have some damned human decency," I conclude.

I see a flicker of emotion in his eye, but it's quickly covered with ice. He leans forward, his mouth inches from my ear. His breath is awful, and his messy, greasy unwashed hair gives off a stench.

"The only people I care about are me and my boys. Damn your sister." he cackles. He is beyond a monster. How could I be so dumb as to try and reason with him? Yet, somehow, he reminds me of...

Bang.

My leg feels like it explodes even before the sound has fully registered.

I drop to ground. My left leg hangs limp off to the side as my right knee holds my body up. The pain is unbearable and I let out a scream. I quickly collect myself and grind my teeth. My mind convinces me that my leg is on fire. As I put pressure on the bleeding hole, the boys laugh and Saul grins like a snake, "I will keep this image in my mind tonight when I take her and I..." All of a sudden, he gasps. I look up for him to finish the sentence, but my eyes lock on to the arrow sticking out from his chest. A red-finned carbon arrow.

No, Caitlyn. They can kill me, but not you.

Saul coughs a mist of blood and stumbles to the ground in front of me. What could be called a scream exits his mouth. The boys behind him look puzzled as they search for her with their guns ready to kill. They begin to yell at one another. Another boy on the lawn drops as an arrow pierces his head. The other one near him points and they all begin shooting at a target somewhere behind me. I reach from my knees and pry Saul's pistol from his hand, which is loose as he focuses on the blood in his lungs. I take aim with his gun and fire three shots. The last boy on the front lawn drops. I take aim at the house and continue to squeeze the trigger, pointing at two of Saul's boys inside a window. Another boy falls and blood covers the wall behind him. We may actually do this. Another boy shooting stares at me; his gun is pointing wherever Caitlyn must be. I take aim. I pull the trigger.

Saul's gun clicks empty, and I swear to myself. He dodges an arrow from Caitlyn and then takes aim at me. The barrel of his gun slowly swings over, lining up with me perfectly. Two explosions engulf my chest, and then I hear the shots. I try to scream in agony, but the muscles in my chest refuse to force the air out of my lungs. All that escapes is an abbreviated yell, fueled by my back striking the side of the tire on the car behind me. I force my eyes open and try to focus on something. Anything. I'm barely sitting up, but I have a clear view of him. He's inside the house and reloading while glaring at me. With the little bit of strength I have left, I reach for my revolver, collapsing away from the tire. It is inches from my hand. I pull together all of my energy, and moan desperately as I reach for the gun.

My fingertips reach the grip.

The boy starts to bring the gun to his shoulder. When my hand clutches the revolver, it is too late. I hear the gun fire.

Behind him an arm comes around with a knife. The blade pierces his chest and a flicker of blood follows the knife as it leaves his body. The boy drops.

Carter stands behind him, panting and clutching the knife; red trickles down the left side of his face. His eyes search the lawn and street.

"That's the last one." he yells. I had not even noticed that that boy was the last one shooting. Carter looks out the shattered window, and he focuses on me. Shock covers his face. He leaps through the window. Behind him I see Jo.

She is safe.

Carter runs to me. I'm not even sure how many times I have been shot. The pool of blood continues to grow around me. It's sticky and warm. It shouldn't be there. Carter leaps over Saul's lifeless body and kneels in the blood. He tries to assess me as he leans me gently against the tire of a car.

"I'm sorry for... for what I said." The words seem to gurgle as they leave my lips. I can no longer draw breath on command. My chest convulses while attempting to inhale and seizes as it realizes that breathing is barely possible.

"Stop talking. I can fix this." Carter yells. I would laugh if I could. With my little strength, I slap his hands away.

His face changes from determined to apologetic as he accepts defeat.

Jo finally catches up. Tears already run from her eyes. She has a few bruises, but she looks okay. "Oh God, Jonathon," she says wiping the blood off of my face. "Carter, do something!"

"There's nothing I can do." She knew that was true before she even said it. Something squeezes my hand. Caitlyn. She still has the bow in her hand. I turn and Sara is a few steps behind her. Both are crying.

"It'll be alright girls. You all will be..." In the distance I hear an engine coming up the road. The Sanctuary's nightly search team perhaps. They are headed back to the base; maybe they heard the shots. They have to come right through here. My cheeks and nose tremble.

I manage to grab Carter's shoulder. "Get them out of here." I need just one more good breath. "You have to get them out of here. The car is just over the hill there."

"You are coming, too." Jo starts to get under my one shoulder to get me up. I fight her attempt to pick me up. The effort is excruciating.

I shake my head, swallowing. "Leave me. When they... when they find these bodies they are gonna start looking. If they manage to find you it's... it's over." My hand shakes as I grab the revolver.

"We aren't leaving you." Sara run up and grabs my hand. She pulls it. "Get up."

"Sara, you need to go. Everything will be okay."

"No it isn't; we need you. We love you." Caitlyn holds Sara from behind, slowly pulling her away. Caitlyn understands.

Jo looks down to me, and I up at her. She will not see me again, but I know she'll be alright. We hold that gaze, and for a moment, my chest relaxes.

"Thank you," she whispers and kisses my forward. "I love you, brother." Carter gives me a nod and takes Jo by the hand.

"I will take care of them." He says. I know he will.

Carter picks up Sara with his other arm and they head over the hill. Sara's sobbing eyes stare at me over his shoulder, just like they had yesterday. My vision is hazy but I think they stop for one last second to look at me. Then, they are gone over the hill. There is a moment of near silence. I see the three dead boys spread over the lawn. The one is so young and I don't feel bad. What has this world turned me into? Maybe this is how it needs to end, before I become a monster.

The roar of the truck gets closer and closer. I bring the gun to my lap. It figures that at the end this would be the last friend with me. I hold it up to the road just as the truck comes around a corner. I squeeze my finger. As the shot echoes, the car stops. I hear them yelling to one another. I squeeze again. They start to shoot back, but they don't see my broken body along the car. I fire again and again.

Then my hand collapses onto the ground, now drenched in my blood, and the guns slides away. I don't have anything left in me. I cough, and I feel so tired. I want all this pain to go away. The boys are shouting to one another, firing shots randomly. I hear them getting closer.

Finally, one of the boys finds me. He calls to the others and in a few hazy blinks, they surround me. None of them fire a shot. I guess I look pretty pathetic.

The first boy stands in front of me with a pistol just like Saul's in his hand, dangling at his side. He has short black hair and is no older than the twins. My neck relaxes, turning my head toward him. I want to say something, but I can't. Everything is blurry.

"I know you; you caused us some pretty serious headaches yesterday." He looks around and sees the bodies, including Saul's. "You just keep causing us problems. Well no more." I feel the cold steel barrel against my forehead. I can hear his finger begin to pull the trigger.

I think of Jo, and those two girls.

I didn't let you down, father. See you soon.

Chapter 36: Jocelyn

Carter pulls at my right hand. I look back over my shoulder and see my brother for the last time. My free hand wipes away the tears. I follow Carter and the twins down over the embankment and into the SUV that is parked along the side of the road. Everyone jumps in the car and Carter slams on the gas. He heads north down the road. I roll the window down to get a little air, only to hear a pop way behind us. Then another. Then a final one that I barely hear over the engine and Sara's cries in the backseat.

Caitlyn pulls her sister's head into her lap and runs her fingers through her hair. When I ran over the front lawn to Jon, I saw the bodies with the red arrows – the same red arrows still in Caitlyn's quiver sitting beside her on the seat. The bow is on top of them. She watches as my eyes go from the bow to her.

"Are you okay?" I whisper to her.

"I'm okay. Why wouldn't I be? I'm not hurt." She blinks at me and seems to look straight through me. I feel a chill. Caitlyn has become a child of this new world; Sara, on the other hand, is struggling.

We remain silent in the car for about another half hour before Carter breaks the silence.

"If we drive through the night, we should be able to be at the beacon by daybreak." I nod and return my gaze to the window. In the back seat, both girls fall asleep.

Carter reaches over and grabs my left hand. I place my right hand on top of his. I stare out the window at the passing houses. I feel so tired but I don't think that I could actually fall asleep. I slowly rub the top of his hand. A few times I have to squeeze his hand to try and push the last image of my brother from my mind. When we are safe I can let it all out.

We drive all night, and few words are shared between any of us. There isn't much to say. Carter doesn't have to say why he came back; I know why.

After a few hours, Carter pulls over to refill the car with the gas cans in the trunk. He pulls out the map to double check our heading.

"We should be there within the hour." He says to me. The girls are asleep in the backseat, but I bet they would be excited, if they could manage excitement after today. We continue our journey down the road. There is not a cloud in the sky and I stare straight up through the moon roof at the stars. At constellations. At heroes.

I wonder if Jon is up there now. The thought makes me smile briefly. It takes a lot of concentrating, but I stop the tears from falling.

"We're here," Carter whispers. The headlights reveal an array of tents and paper scattered throughout a giant mall parking lot. We drive past a collapsed sign that reads "UN Emergency Relief and Relocation." It's weird seeing a place that should have so much life look like a wasteland. Carter pulls between the tents and a giant helipad constructed on the corner of a parking lot leading to the mall. On the other side of the helipad are a few trees that become denser as they turn into a forest. He puts the car in park, and I look through the windows. It looks abandoned.

"Where is everybody?" Sara asks. The twins must have woken up.

Carter reaches behind his back and pulls out a gun. He checks the magazine.

"Jo, switch to the driver side. I am going to go check things out. If anything happens. Get out of here. I will meet up with you back down the road. After that, you know the drill: I have fifteen minutes to get to you before you head back to the cabin." It bothers me how nonchalantly he describes his plan in case he dies, too. I'm tired of being told what to do if people don't come back. I can't lose anyone else today.

He opens the door and walks out, his gun up and ready. Carter shouts, "Hey, is there anyone here?" He waits. "We are peaceful; we were told we could come here for help." Still no response. I watch him walking around in the headlights. After spiraling around, observing the area, he disappears behind a tent.

The girls and I hold our breath. One minute goes by. Another minute goes by. Then a third. I feel my pulse quickening.

Without warning the lights come on in the car. The door has opened. I turn into the back seat and the door is already slamming shut. Sara is back there alone. I watch from the car as Caitlyn goes running out, bow at the ready.

"Caitlyn, get back in here!" I yell out my rolled down window. She ignores me and disappears into the night. More minutes go by. Terror is in me. I open the glove compartment and pull out the knife I acquired from what feels like decades ago. When I sit back up I see two figures moving back toward the car.

It is Carter and Caitlyn.

When Carter's and my eyes meet, he shrugs his shoulders and says "I guess it's empty. Grab the flashlights. We can at least see if there is anything we can use." Sara goes into the back and pulls out a few of our lamps. I hand them out and we begin exploring the deserted post.

Chapter 37: Carter

If the UN was here, they have not been here anytime recently. The first tent looks like it had been some sort of medical center. Papers still slowly drifted around the tent. I grab a clipboard from the table. It seems to be an observation of a plague victim. The date on the paper is about two months old. It was done by a doctor. There are a few body bags in the tent, but thankfully they were all twisted and empty.

"Carter, you need to check this out." Jocelyn calls from the nearby tent. I see her silhouette from her flashlight and make my way over to her. She is standing beside a radio. She hands me a bright red piece of paper. This tent is filled with them. On it are directions to call out. I begin to read it aloud.

"Due to unforeseen circumstances, we have relocated to a more secure location. If you are here to seek help and relocation please follow these directions. Security is not far away." Beneath the note is a procedure. The first is to start the generator, dial to a certain frequency on the radio, and give the coordinates, "ECHO 67," then describe your party. After that, we should hear a response and help will arrive.

We follow the directions. The generator still has gas and it roars to life with a few pulls of the chord. Jocelyn picks up the communicator. "This is site ECHO 67. There are four of us that need help. Among us are two young girls and they really need to get out of this mess."

Silence answers her. Then a muffled voice comes back, "We will be there within the hour. Good to see you are safe. Don't worry, they will be out soon."

The twins are standing at the opening of the tent when they hear the response and big smiles light up both of their faces. I smile back. I squeeze Jocelyn's hand, still holding onto the communicator. We share a smile. On the ground is a video camcorder; it's pink and seems out of place. I pick it up. There's a note taped to it that says, "PLAY ME!" I press the power button. It seems dead as it flickers for only a second.

"You girls want to see if you can find some batteries? Don't go far." I give them something to do and walk with Jocelyn back to the SUV. I parked it next to the landing zone they had created in the parking lot. Both of us sit against the back tire facing the helipad. Our hands intertwine and I see the girls to the right running in and out of the various tents. They are opening boxes and stray packs. I close my eyes for a few moments and breathe deeply. I feel at ease. We are almost safe.

The sun begins to rise over the treetops. The helicopter should be here any moment. I sit beside the SUV, Jocelyn's hand in mine. The twins are rummaging through some boxes in one of the nearby tents. I look into her eyes. She has been through so much. I lean forward and our lips meet for a moment. When I pull away I brush her hair behind her left ear.

"We are going to be okay." I tell her.

"I know, thank you for everything." She manages a smile and looks away. Her face is powdered with dirt and the water from her tears shows the flawless skin underneath. She reaches back and pulls her long red hair up for a moment with both hands. She exhales and lets it fall behind her. That is why I came back. I smile and look forward. Sara is running toward me with her hand stretched out in front and grasping a small box.

"Carter I found some batteries that should work in that camera." She pulls out two AA's.

"Thanks." I take them from her and pull the camera from the driver's seat. She goes and sits in Jocelyn's lap. Caitlin comes over and sits on the ground beside me. I put the batteries in and hit play.

I hold it out as the screen lights up. A little blond girl and a dog play on a front lawn. They look happy. The dog rolls around as the girl holds out some sort of stuffed animal. I feel the tension escape the four of us. Sara gives out a little laugh and Jocelyn squeezes her tighter. Caitlin puts her head on my shoulder. The scene changes and then the same girl and a man, her father I guess, open up presents in front of a Christmas tree. The dog runs in and then rolls among the wrapping paper, but the screen suddenly goes black.

"Well I guess that's it..." I am about to switch it off but then a boy's face pops on the screen. He may be fourteen or fifteen years old. His face is dirty and he is breathing loudly. His eyes dart to each side of his face. He begins to talk.

"Whoever you are, you need to run. Now."

Chapter 38: Walter

"I repeat you need to get out of there now. My friends came to this location on September 2nd. We were told that there would be safety by these people who would come to save us. I was the smart one and didn't trust people that just help others. People don't just help. So I hid myself away when the "UN" came to save our group. They didn't listen to me; I told them to hide. But no – let's not listen to Walter." I start to laugh. I don't know why but this is all so funny. The irony of it all that I would be the most clever of them. I guess this is what they deserve for believing in hope. Pulling the dead girl's camera to my mouth, I continue.

"As I peered out from the locker I watched as my friends greeted the helicopters with open arms. Those fools. I almost revealed myself from my hiding place to yell but then I heard the first screams from Caleb, the oldest of our group." Eighteen years old is the oldest. That's funny. The oldest is a senior in high school. We put our hope in a senior in high school. My God, are we stupid. I would have been better staying with sick mom and dad. Their bodies would have given better advice than Caleb, the damned neighbor.

"Caleb had been injured in an explosion while trying to siphon gas out of a car." Smoking can be so dangerous – especially when I leave the cigarette in the wrong place. "When the men in the helicopters saw his injuries they pulled out a gun and executed him." I still see the mess that shot left. I finally got to see all that intelligence out in the open. Not a lot of intelligence.

"Then they separated the children from the group. The really young children were loaded into one helicopter and then another. I watched as they tore a baby from Juliette's arms as they slammed the doors to the chopper shut." I guess they don't like babies too much... good thing I am not one. "A few men did a poor search of the perimeter and then the helicopters took off. I emerged from the locker and watched as the helicopters flew away. I don't know who these people are but they aren't exactly the UN Aid that was promised in the radio transmissions."

"I grabbed this camera from a nearby corpse and thought I'd warn ya. Hopefully you didn't go calling for help. Oh well, your funeral!" My thumb pushes the red button. I set it on the radio receiver.

What to do. What to do. What to do?

I rummage through everyone's packs and take the best goods ever so carefully. They tried to hide the stuff that "mattered." They said they couldn't trust me when I ran out of my pills.

Well look who is still free. Would a madman be so clever to outsmart men in black helicopters?

I turn to the forest.

Time to have some fun.

Chapter 39: Caitlyn

The screen goes black. All of us quickly rise to our feet.

"What are we going do?" Jocelyn pleads frantically to Carter. I can already hear the helicopters on the way. Jocelyn always seemed frantic about something and it's beginning to get to me. She needed to calm down.

"We don't even know if that's real, Jo. Do you see all this official United Nation stuff lying around? How could they not be here to help? The kid seemed liked he lost it. Did you hear his laugh and that look in his eyes?" Carter started to yell as the engines and blades of the approaching helicopters drown out our voices.

"I think Carter is right. If there is a chance to go to a normal life I want it," Sara joins in. She yells, too. I don't know who to believe. It's too late anyway. The helicopters are landing right on the big "H" that isn't too far away. We wouldn't get far if we were to run now.

The doors on the helicopters slam open. Men in gas masks and assault rifles jump out. They point them all at us. I think Carter was wrong.

"Get down on the ground!" They scream. All of our hands go up and we begin to lie down. Carter stays standing and walks towards the soldier. The men continue to yell, "Is anyone injured?"

"No one is hurt. We are cool man; we are just looking for help..." Carter's reply is cut short when one hits him in the stomach with the butt of his gun. Sara screams. One of the men grabs her and yells at her to shut up. She keeps screaming. He hits her across the face with his hand. She goes limp.

Before I know it, I am on top of the nearest soldier kicking and biting him. "Let her go." I scream. Jocelyn struggles but one of the men has her two arms and is dragging her to the nearer chopper. Some blood leaks from Carter's mouth as two men carry him to the same chopper.

"Leave them alone!" Jocelyn screams. She is thrown in. Carter is hoisted in behind her and the door to the helicopter is slammed shut.

They keep trying to get hold of me. I feel light headed as the man keeps hitting my head. He finally manages to pick me up under his arm.

"Sara!" I yell as she is loaded into the other helicopter. The other one is taking off and I see Jocelyn banging on the window out at us. A gloved hand quickly covers her mouth and pulls her back.

My vision becomes blurry. I stop kicking and screaming. It isn't working anyway. They carry me to right in front of the helicopter. The one holding me and one in front of him are the only ones in front of the chopper.

How did all this happen? We were so close to safety. This meant everything to them.

Then I see my opportunity: the soldier's knife hanging off his gear on his chest. I look up at his mask covered face, finding a seam by his neck. He seems to be ignoring me; he thinks I am out like my sister.

I grab his knife and thrust it under his mask and into his neck. He falls without a yell. As he collapses, my feet find the ground. With the knife in hand, I charge to the nearby woods at the other end of the helipad parking lot. Those men won't be happy when they notice who I've killed.

As I get to the dense trees, the bark beside me splinters away and I hear the shots beneath the sound of the helicopters. The masked men are shooting at me. I keep running until I find an old, withered tree and climb behind it. The shots spread throughout the trees around me.

I peek out after a few moments go by without any gunshots. The second helicopter is taking off. They must not want me that badly.

Sara. I feel sadness sweep over me, but this is no time to cry.

I watch the helicopters flying into the sun, east. Soon they are out of sight. I come out of the forest and go to the dead soldier. His mask is now off, so I see who I killed. Maybe I should feel sadness for this, but I feel nothing. He has a cell phone clipped to his belt. I take it. I open it and it has service. What's more, it has a full battery. Somehow I feel lucky at this moment.

I walk to the car, grabbing my backpack with my bow and arrows. The helicopters did not take long to get here after we called. They cannot be too far. I look up at the rising sun and tuck the soldier's knife into my backpack.

Swinging my gear over my shoulders, I run into the forest. I have killed four people in the last several hours – not bad for a twelve year old. I will kill as many as it takes to get my family back– especially to get Sara back.

End of Book I

Humanity Gone

Thank You

Both of us appreciate your time and hope you enjoyed book I of the *Humanity Gone* Saga. "After the Plague" is an accumulation of original and "borrowed" ideas from throughout my life. Over a year ago, I started a rough outline of the story on a piece of sketch paper. It was partially inspired by O.T. Nelson's *The Girl Who Owned a City*, a book I read way back in middle school. A world without supervision always held a certain appeal to me. However, in his book the magic age was 12. I wanted to up the ante and incorporate young adults. Young children can be mean, but young adults could be barbaric.

The concept of shifting perspectives stems from several sources. In my mind, I wanted something between K.A. Applegate's *Animorphs* series, and George R.R. Martin's *A Song of Ice and Fire* series. That could be the first time those two works have ever been compared. The presentation was also meant to be cinematic in a sense by relying on dramatic irony in key moments across the story.

Originally this started as a solo project for the first several months until I realized that I needed help as it grew into a real pandemic of sorts. I enlisted Dean to help with editing, but soon found him to have invaluable ideas of his own that have been incorporated throughout the work.

After the initial manuscript was finished, we bounced drafts back and forth. I was lucky to even have author Jay Wilburn add his two cents at the revision stage, and I thank him for his thorough critical response.

As I write this, Dean is doing a hunt for typos and grammar errors. He texts me that he is exhausted. I am too. We have managed to pass it back and forth several times already, but somehow the occasional homonym or a Dickinson-like use of a dash rears its ugly head. My birthday (and speaking of Emily Dickinson- hers as well) is in a half hour and I hope to have sent it sometime tomorrow for finalizing. However, I know I will not let it go until I give it one last read through.

I guess this is why God made publishing companies.

Yet, we stuck it to the "publishing man" and made this product that we are both very proud of accomplishing, and I hope you join us on our next adventure.

Book II is in the works. The plague is in the past; now it's time to see who takes control. Thanks again.

Derek Deremer
12/9/2012

About the Authors

Derek Deremer

Derek Deremer is currently an English teacher in South Carolina. He somehow wandered down there after growing up in the suburbs of Pittsburgh. While graduating with an English degree from Westminster College, he developed his love for common words and many other endeavors in his continual pursuit to be a jack of all trades and a master of none.

Dean Culver

Dean Culver is an engineer and scientist, pursuing amateur ventures in many fields both within and beyond the borders of science and technology. Born, raised, and currently residing in Pittsburgh, he has occasionally traveled and relocated, hoping to find where his goal of creative balance can be achieved.

Made in the USA
Charleston, SC
07 January 2013